TEMPORARY DUTY

Wade Everett, a pseudonym for Will Cook, is the author of numerous outstanding Western novels as well as historical frontier fiction. He was born in Richmond, Indiana, but was raised by an aunt and uncle in Cambridge, Illinois. He joined the U.S. cavalry at the age of sixteen but was disillusioned because horses were being eliminated through mechanization. He transferred to the U.S. Army Air Force in which he served in the South Pacific during the Second World War. Cook turned to writing in 1951 and contributed a number of outstanding short stories to *Dime Western* and other pulp magazines as well as fiction for major smooth-paper magazines such as *The Saturday Evening Post*. It was in the *Post* that his best-known novel, *Comanche Captives*, was serialized. It was later filmed as *Two Rode Together* (Columbia, 1961) directed by John Ford and starring James Stewart and Richard Widmark. It has now been restored, as was the author's intention, with *The Peacemakers* set in 1870 as the first part and *Comanche Captives* set in 1874 as the second part of a major historical novel titled *Two Rode Together*. Sometimes in his short stories Cook would introduce characters that would later be featured in novels, such as Charlie Boomhauer who first appeared in *Lawmen Die Sudden* in *Big-Book Western* in 1953 and is later to be found in *Badman's Holiday* (1958) and *The Wind River Kid* (1958). Along with his steady productivity, Cook maintained an enviable quality. His novels range widely in time and place, from the Illinois frontier of 1811 to southwest Texas in 1905, but each is peopled with credible and interesting characters whose interactions form the backbone of the narrative. Most of his novels deal with more or less traditional Western themes—range wars, reformed outlaws, cattle rustling, Indian fighting—but there are also romantic novels such as *Sabrina Kane* (1956) and exercises in historical realism such as *Elizabeth, by Name* (1958). Indeed, his fiction is known for its strong heroines. Another common feature is Cook's compassion for his characters who must be able to survive in a wild and violent land. His protagonists make mistakes, hurt people they care for, and sometimes succumb to ignoble impulses, but this all provides an added dimension to the artistry of his work.

TEMPORARY DUTY

Wade Everett

GUNSMOKE

First published in the UK by Collins

This hardback edition 2012
by AudioGO Ltd
by arrangement with
Golden West Literary Agency

ISBN 978 1 445 85084 9

British Library Cataloguing in Publication Data available.

Printed and bound in Great Britain by
MPG Books Group Limited

THEY were married as soon as he got his assignment: Arizona Territory, in the year 1864, and they were both happy about it. His name was Linus McCaffey, and he was twenty-five, already with two years of duty behind him, and a mention in a dispatch for his efficiency. This was a word that galled him for he had hoped it would be bravery, or at least devotion to duty, but not efficiency.

He was cavalry, but somehow he had been closed out of a company command and given instead a job in regiment where he juggled papers and added columns of figures and made sure that enough forage and ammunition reached the trooper at just the right time.

Because he had made no mistakes, he was cited for his efficiency.

Her name was Eloise Finnerty, but now it was McCaffey, and she had no complaints for she had plotted this marriage since she had been seven and Linus had stolen her shoe and thrown it in the mud. And afterward, her father, who had been a Baltimore policeman, took Linus by the ear and marched him to his father, who gave him a strapping there on the front steps and she had cried more than he because she had loved him and had brought about his shame and downfall.

Tucson was their destination and the spring weather was hot and dust kept boiling into the stage through the open windows and he kept reassuring her that this condition was only temporary, and she tried not to complain and be a burden to him.

McCaffey was a dark, bold-faced man, rather thin, like

5

a good cutting horse. He carried himself in the miltary manner, as though he had been brought to attention so often that he couldn't quite bring himself to relax. The details of his uniform marked him as coming from a middle-class family; his blouse had been tailormade, yet was not of fine fabric, pointing to a limited allowance. His sword had cost seventy-five dollars, and was not a Castellani, although it had come from the forge of a good, but lesser-known maker.

Eloise McCaffey was twenty, a dark-haired, deep blue-eyed, fresh-cheeked twenty, and beneath her flowing traveling dress was a figure neither too many children nor too many potatoes had spoiled.

The coach was crowded; McCaffey and his wife sat together, with a cattleman beside him, a tradesman across, knees barely touching his, and two drummers, all Tucson bound.

The cattleman drank from a bottle and one of the drummers smoked one horrible cigar after the other, and Eloise McCaffey kept closing her eyes and putting her head on her husband's shoulder, and finally he tapped the drummer on the knee.

"Will you stop smoking those blasted things? It's stifling enough in here."

The man looked at his cigar, then at Linus McCaffey, and said, "They don't bother me."

Using the butt of his sword, McCaffey tapped on the roof of the coach and the driver sawed the team to a halt. McCaffey got down and the drummer, knowing why they had stopped, got down and McCaffey promptly knocked the man flat, picked him up, and sprawled him in the dust again. Then he took the man's cigars out of his pocket and threw them away, and afterward helped him back into the coach. The driver had observed this with detachment, and he drove on.

When the cattleman started to take another swig out of his bottle, he noticed McCaffey's eyes on him and after hesitating, he corked it and put it in his coat pocket, resigning himself to a dry trip.

Tucson was a pueblo and little more, and Eloise had

difficulty hiding her disappointment in not finding a good hotel with a bath available. A corporal met them with an ambulance and drove them to the post and showed them their quarters, a two-room apartment in a long row of apartments.

The furniture was poor, sparse, and the walls were adobe, calcimined white, and the bed was lumpy, narrow, and protested loudly when weight was put on it.

As a second lieutenant, McCaffey didn't get much in the way of a striker. Private Noonan had spent more time in the stockade than on duty, and when he presented himself at the door, he was unshaven, out of uniform, and smelled of stale beer.

"Bring a tub and four buckets of water," McCaffey said.

Noonan put a finger under his forager cap and pursued a louse that was pestering him. "Lootenant, all the water's got to be hauled on the post."

McCaffey's irritation crept into his voice. "I'm not concerned with the source of it, or how it gets here. Just bring me four buckets and a tub and don't be long doing it." He closed the door and went into the bedroom and began to take off his blouse. Eloise had removed her heavy dress and was stretched out on the bed, clad in her shift and Linus McCaffey, who was still new to married life, tried not to look too pointedly at her.

He said, "I'm sorry, dear. About the heat and the dust and this miserable place. I don't know what I expected on the frontier, but better than this."

"It's only temporary duty," she said.

"Yes," he said, feeling relieved. "It's only temporary."

Private Noonan brought the water and tub and much later, after they had bathed and Linus had changed into a fresh uniform, he went to report to his new commanding officer.

Captain Paul Lovering commanded the military at the Tucson post; he was a gaunt, seasoned man who had accepted this post rather than retirement after losing an arm at Vicksburg. At forty, his hair was nearly all gray and deep lines ran across his forehead when he frowned.

"I trust you had a perfectly miserable journey, Mr. McCaffey. They all do. Sit down. We don't stand on formalities here." He offered McCaffey a cigar, then realized the young man had few vices. "That'll change," Lovering said.

McCaffey said, "I beg your pardon, sir?"

"Sorry. Habit. Answering my own mental speculations. Mr. McCaffey, General Beaumont wrote me a letter highly recommending you to this duty." He drew a map from the desk drawer and spread it. "Department of Platte has authorized a new division, the Department of Arizona. We are to construct and occupy four military posts in the next four years. Mr. McCaffey, you're going to build those forts for me."

"I was under the impression that I would be given tactical duty," McCaffey said.

"Nonsense," Lovering said. "You stood at the head of your class in mathematics. General Beaumont speaks highly of your staff work and grasp on logistics." He smiled. "I intend to use native labor, so the job may not be as uninteresting as you imagine."

"Natives, sir? Indians?"

"Good God, no! Whites, and in some way, worse than Indians." He put his map away. "We'll have a meeting in the morning, Mr. McCaffey. In the meantime, I trust you and your wife will dine with us tonight. My wife will be hungry for any news from back East."

"I'm sure my wife will be delighted," McCaffey said and left the captain's office. The heat of the day was stronger, he noticed as he crossed the small parade ground. A most dismal post, he concluded, constructed on a sandy, cactus-covered plot, backed by a mountain range that was forbidding. There was about the camp a suggestion that it had first been built for some other purpose and later modified for military use.

When McCaffey returned to his quarters he found the trunks and boxes he had shipped a month early piled by his door with Noonan comfortably asleep on them. McCaffey shook him awake and said, "You could have taken those inside for my wife."

"She told me to go take a bath," he said. "Lootenant, that's gettin' kind of personal, ain't it?"

"It sounds like a good suggestion. Why didn't you?"

He shrugged. "Well, sir, I just got out of jail and they didn't have nothin' for me to do, so they assigned me to you."

"You mean that no company would have you."

"If you want to put it that way, I guess so. Are you goin' to report me for not mindin' your missus?"

Eloise heard the talking and opened the door. McCaffey said, "Private Noonan doesn't like us. He wants me to send him back to headquarters for punishment."

"Why, that's silly," she said. "Why haven't you bathed yet?"

"He is about to," McCaffey said firmly.

Noonan got to his feet. "Now wait a minute—"

McCaffey grabbed him around the neck and locked him that way, hurting him a little, but dragging him in tow across the parade to the watering trough. The enlisted men saw this and a crowd formed as they reached the trough, then McCaffey threw Noonan over his hip so that he landed in the water.

"Fetch me some soap and a brush," he said to no one in particular, and three men dashed off for these items, eager to supply the tools for a good show.

Noonan struggled and McCaffey managed to hold him in the water until he had soap and brush and got his own uniform wet in the process. He had help in getting Noonan's clothes off, and two enlisted men volunteered to help scrub him, then Captain Lovering came striding through the gathering.

"What the blazes is going on here?" he demanded.

"Giving my striker a bath, sir," McCaffey said.

Lovering looked at Noonan, lathered and spitting mad, and hid his smile. "Carry on," he said and returned to his headquarters.

When the job was finished, McCaffey threw soap and brush in the trough and stepped back while Noonan glared and the others roared with laughter. Noonan was too much of a soldier to say anything, but he glared at McCaffey before he turned and walked away.

His wife was waiting and she scolded him. "Oh, just look at your clothes. What were you trying to prove, Linus?"

"That a man does his duty whether he likes it or not," he said, and went into the bedroom to change. Then he discovered that he had no other uniform pressed.

"You should have thought of that before you gave him a bath," Eloise said. "Here, let me try and dry it for you. My, you're going to create an impression at the captain's dinner tonight."

"The heat ought to dry—" He looked at her. "Who mentioned the captain's dinner?"

"It was in that book you gave me when we were married," she said. "How to be a proper officer's wife."

He took off his wet blouse and hung it over the back of a chair. "I suppose I ought to get those trunks and crates inside. I thought I had another clean uniform. Or was that the one I spilled coffee on?"

"It was red wine," she said, "and you spilled it the night you celebrated your new assignment."

He went to her and put his arms around her and smiled down at her and said, "Eloise, how long have I been married to you now?"

She put her finger against her cheek and made a big thing of thinking about it. "Forty-eight days, if I'm not mistaken."

"No, I've been married to you forever, since I was a small boy." He kissed her lightly. "I don't think there was ever a moment of doubt in your mind that I'd one day marry you."

"Why, you proposed to me! What a thing to say!"

"Either way," he said, "it's a wonderful thing. You're wonderful and I want life to be good to you. Thank God this duty is only temporary. I may be able to draw a decent post where you can have a decent home when this one is finished."

"Now you do your work, Second Lieutenant Linus

McCaffey, and don't worry whether I've got everything you think I ought to have. Mother learned to raise six children on a policeman's pay, so I'll manage on yours." She pulled back and patted her hair in place. "Tonight, be sure and ask the captain if he's ever known Tad. The last letter mother got was in '62 and he was in the Colorado Volunteers then."

"I won't forget," McCaffey said. "But it was damned inconsiderate of him not to stay home and become a policeman like your other brothers." He smiled. "Your geography's bad. Colorado is a long way from Arizona Territory."

"Well, it won't hurt to ask," she said. "Now let's see if I can do anything with the blouse you all but ruined."

She built a fire in the stove and he stepped out to get the trunks in; she had a flatiron in one of them and he'd have to unpack to find it.

Private Noonan approached the porch as McCaffey unbuckled the straps. Noonan wore a clean uniform, one that still bore the unmistakable wrinkles of the quartermaster's shelf.

He said, "You did a fine job of shamin' me in front of the men, sir."

McCaffey looked at him. "Seems to me you did that before I came here. Don't you have any pride left? What ever happens to a man to make him a guardhouse bum?" He saw that Noonan wasn't going to give him an answer. "Give me a hand with these blasted trunks."

"Lootenant, I don't understand you. I could be carryin' a grudge for all you know."

"Carry one then," McCaffey said. "Isn't life tough enough for you? Do you have to add to it? Now get hold of that end there and let's get these into my quarters. You might as well make up your mind that I'm not turning you in for discipline."

They took the trunks and boxes inside and Eloise supervised the opening of them and had Noonan carry this into the bedroom and that over in the corner; the sweat began to stand out on his forehead.

McCaffey said, "Now you see what married life is

like." He smiled and his wife stuck her tongue out at him, but Noonan let the humor pass him completely.

"I already knew what it was like," he said and went on with his work There was no attempt made to really set the quarters in order, but when the trunks and boxes were unpacked, Noonan took them to the storage shed and afterward went to his barracks.

While they were dressing for Captain Lovering's dinner, Eloise said, "Are you going to keep that private on, Linus?"

"Yes," McCaffey said. "He'll be all right once we get to understand each other."

"He seems moody." She turned her back to him. "Hook me up."

McCaffey concentrated on this chore. "Somehow I distrust a man I can see through. Noonan's a problem to the post and probably he will be to me. But I rather like the man, rebellion and all." He gave her rounded rump a slap. "There. That dress is so tight you won't be able to eat anything. You're not getting fat, are you?"

2

No SUITABLE ACCOMMODATIONS existed on the post, so Captain Lovering and his wife lived in Tucson. An ambulance carried them into town and after his second look at the squat adobes and the dust Mc-Caffey was unimpressed. Lovering's adobe sat on a side street and a gaunt tree tried to survive in his yard.

"There's really nothing here to build with except mud," he said as he got down and offered Eloise his hand. "However, once it bakes hard, it's virtually indestructible."

The captain ushered them inside and introduced his wife, a tall woman in her middle thirties, with dark hair and a complexion easily ruined by harsh sunlight. There were only three rooms in the adobe; the kitchen was an L built on, and the women went there while Lovering and McCaffey sat down with their cigars.

"The thick walls help keep out the heat," Lovering said. "Which is some blessing, I suppose. Adobe will be your main source of building material, Mr. McCaffey. However, there will be some native woods available. The site selected for the post is fifty some miles from town. There was once a settlement there, so some buildings remain, although they are in a miserable state of decay. I know you're anxious to ride out and take a look, and perhaps we can get at it day after tomorrow."

McCaffey puffed on his cigar, gently so as not to begin coughing. "I don't suppose there will be accommodations for my wife."

"Out of the question," Lovering said. "Perhaps in a

few months." He laughed softly. "The situation will only be temporary, McCaffey."

"That's some reassurance," McCaffey said. "But with my wife on the post, I suppose she'll be—"

"I'm afraid we can't do that," Lovering said. "The place was once a stage station and trading post and our accommodations at best are limited. You might find some place here in town. Rent's rather high, but as I said, the situation is only—"

"Yes, I know. Temporary."

The meal was both a success and a failure, depending upon the point of view. Elizabeth Lovering used every bit of ingenuity at her command to turn beef and beans into a meal with some social grace, and to her way of thinking, she succeeded. McCaffey, new to the frontier, thought that it would have failed to pass any mess sergeant's eye on a first-class post. But he was a polite man and never revealed this.

Afterward they went to the parlor with their coffee and talked about Tucson and the Indians, always a bother, and how this situation was only temporary and would rapidly improve as soon as decent posts were built.

McCaffey took the ambulance back to the post and left word for someone to go into town and pick the captain up in the morning. In his own quarters, he sat down to take off his boots while his wife struggled out of her dress.

"No one has very much here, do they?" she said. "I mean, the poor woman didn't have a decent set of dishes, really."

"They probably got broken on the way here," he said. "I'll have to find a place in town for you to live tomorrow." She looked at him steadily. "Well, I can't take you with me. The captain was firm enough about that." He removed his trousers and hung them up so they wouldn't get wrinkled. "Anyway, it isn't so far that I can't ride back to Tucson now and then."

He waited until she got into bed, then blew out the lamp and settled beside her. She came against him and he put his arm around her, and held her for a time. Then she said, "Linus, I'm not afraid."

"That's good," he said and kissed her gently.

Shortly after reveille, Private Noonan brought a box of rations to McCaffey's quarters; without it they would have had nothing to eat for breakfast, and over Noonan's protest, McCaffey insisted that he stay and have a cup of coffee.

Afterward, Noonan saddled two horses and they rode into Tucson where McCaffey wasted over half the day looking for a house, and settled finally on a two-room adobe belonging to a saloon keeper. The rent was eighteen dollars a month, more than he had intended to pay, but the town was growing and places were hard to find, so he made the deal and sent Noonan back to the post for a wagon and their belongings. When Noonan returned, he had a message from Captain Lovering, who was ready to leave and wanted McCaffey back on the post. He found it difficult to leave his new wife in a new house, in a strange town with crates and trunks scattered about, but this was the army and they would both have to make the best of it.

As soon as Joe Noonan returned to the post, Eloise McCaffey stood in the middle of the room and looked around, trying to find a place to start. She knew what she had to do and got her purse and braved the scalding sunlight and walked to the center of town and the general store. There seemed, she thought, a sparsity of women in the store, but supposed that the heat of the day kept them inside. The storekeeper was waiting on a tall, well-dressed man who wore a pearl-handled pistol and an air of arrogance; his glance came her way when she approached the counter and the man smiled in appreciation. Then he went outside and Eloise McCaffey placed her order.

"I want a scrub pail, some strong soap, five pounds of calcimine, and a brush."

"Little housecleanin'?"

"A lot of housecleaning," she said. "When a woman has a problem where to start, she picks on the dirt."

"My wife's the same way," the storekeeper said. "New to Tucson, ain't you?"

"Yes. My husband's in the army. Lieutenant Mc-Caffey."

"George Twilling's my name. Got the best store in town."

She smiled. "Isn't it the only store?"

"That's why it's the best," Twilling said.

He sold her a mop and carried the things to the door for her. The well-dressed man with the pistol was standing to one side and he looked her way and smiled again. George Twilling said, "Did you forget something, Dan?"

"I can stand here if I want," the man said. "Besides, I'm waiting for brother Al." He looked past Twilling in the other direction. "Here he comes now."

At first, Eloise didn't recognize the man, then she placed him, the heavy smoker on the stage. He recognized her also and smiled. "Where's your husband? Busy putting out cigars?" He glanced at his brother. "She's married to the guy I was telling you about. He jumped me before I knew what happened."

"So you said." He looked at Eloise McCaffey and smiled. "I'm anxious to meet your husband. Al's kind of puny. Doesn't do too well with his fists."

"He does all right with his mouth," she said. "And if he says that Linus jumped him, he lies."

The man frowned. "Honey, the Gannons don't lie. They don't let people say they do either." He tapped her with his finger, but only once, for she slapped his hand away. He looked at her and then at his hand and said, "I was only going to drive home a point."

"Don't," she said. "Now good day. I have more to do than stand here and talk to someone I don't like." She turned and took a step and Al grabbed her by the arm and she whirled as though by reflex and lopped him alongside the head with the wooden pail. He pitched off the walk and into the dust and sat there, half stunned.

The brother opened his mouth to say something, and

she broke the five pound paper bag of calcimine over his head. He coughed and stamped and cursed in a rank cloud, and George Twilling pulled her toward the door.

The men along the street saw all this and they began to gather. Twilling said, "Inside's the place for you." He herded her along and then got his shotgun from beneath the counter and faced the door. None too soon for both men started inside, but stopped when they saw Twilling and the shotgun.

Dan said, "You really shouldn't stick your nose in this, George."

"I am," he said, "because you're sticking your nose in. Now get out of my store, Dan Gannon. Take your brother with you."

"This isn't finished," Al Gannon said. "Wait 'til her husband shows up." They turned and went on down the street and George Twilling put his shotgun away.

"Too bad your husband had to run afoul of the Gannon boys," he said. "This here little affair won't help none either."

"What did you expect me to do?" she asked.

"Just what you did." He grinned. "I'll fetch you a new bucket and some calcimine. On the house."

A Mexican boy carried the bucket and package to her house and she gave him two pennies and he ran down the street, calling to his brothers to see his new fortune. There was water to carry and the work was hard and she lost herself in it and it was nearly dark before she realized she had no kerosene for her lamps. Rather than go back to the store she decided to borrow from her neighbor; a rather large, rambling adobe was situated barely fifty yards away across a vacant lot.

She went there and knocked and finally a woman answered the door. She looked at Eloise McCaffey and said, "What do you want?"

"I don't have any kerosene for my lamp and I wondered if I might borrow some."

The woman hesitated, then nodded and stepped back from the door. Eloise went inside and waited and another woman came out. She looked curiously at Eloise, then said, "I heard May talking. You'd better get out of here before Bessie wakes up."

"Who's Bessie?"

A heavy step came from a rear hall, then a fat, hard-eyed woman came into the room. "Did I hear my name mentioned? Better get ready, Emma. Be havin' company soon." She looked at Eloise.

"Who're you?"

"Eloise McCaffey, your new neighbor. I came to borrow—"

The other woman came back with a gallon can. "Here's your coal oil." Then she saw Bessie and hurriedly explained. "She just wanted it for her lamp and—"

"I know what it's for, lamps and curing lice," Bessie said. "Honey, do you know what this place is?"

Eloise McCaffey looked around the room, then at the women, then said, "Oh, dear."

Bessie laughed. "The customers are going to be showing up soon, so you'd better get out of here before they think I've got a new girl. Go on, get out of here and don't come back."

Eloise backed to the door and opened it. "Thank you for the—"

"To hell with that," Bessie said. "Get out of here."

She went to her adobe with the coal oil and filled her lamps, and while she fixed herself a simple supper, she thought of Bessie and her neighbors. From the window she could see the growing traffic to Bessie's door, and she jumped when someone knocked on her own.

"Who is it?"

"George Twilling. Brung my missus with me."

She let them in and womanlike, apologized for the condition of the room and the smell of the drying calcimine. Mrs. Twilling was a grave-faced woman who found little to smile about in Tucson.

"It wasn't until later that I found out where you lived," Twilling said. "I hope you won't be bothered none." He had a package under his arm and unwrapped it, then laid the sawed-off shotgun on a box. "There's nothing like one of these to give a woman comfort when her man's away. All you got to do is cock the hammers and pull the triggers. I loaded it with buckshot for you."

"Well I hardly think I'll need—"

"Never can tell," Twilling said, interrupting her. "My wife carries a little two-shot all the time. Don't you, lamb?"

"This town is full of men who can't leave a white woman alone," Mrs. Twilling said, twitching her nose. "Why, I've been molested on the main street, haven't I, George?"

"So you've said, lamb." He smiled. "Well, I only wanted to see that you got the shotgun. If there's anything I can do, or if you need help, you just follow this street way to the end. Our place is the last adobe on the left, right at the edge of town."

"I'm sure I'll be all right," Eloise said. "And I'm not afraid."

"Such innocence," Mrs. Twilling said. "It reminds me so of my own youth. Doesn't it, George?"

"If you say so, lamb," Twilling said. "Hope your husband gets back soon. It's no town for a woman alone, white skin or dark."

They left and she locked her door and made up the bed. The furniture was crudely made, and there wasn't much of it, other than the table, three chairs, the bed, and a bureau someone had made out of packing crates. The work left her tired and she soon put out the lamp and sat down on the bed to unbutton her shoes. Bessie's place was a riot of noise, the laughter loud and strong. Someone played a banjo badly and the dancing went on for hours, keeping her awake, or waking her when she dozed.

Much later, the sudden shock of gunfire woke her and she fumbled for the shotgun on the chair beside her bed. She sat up in bed, breathing heavily, her heart pounding.

A mounted man raced past her door while other men shouted after him and another shot was fired, the bullet striking the wall of her house. Then it fell quiet and a woman was crying, and she slowly settled back on the bed, a slight trembling starting first in her fingers, then running all over her.

George Twilling was right; it was a lonesome, frightening town for a woman alone, and she thought: Linus, no matter where you are tonight, being with you would be better than this.

The night ended and a dawn light came through the window and rinsed out the blackness and before it was really full daylight she made a fire in the sheet iron stove and cooked her breakfast.

When she looked out, the sun was up and Tucson lay quiet, like some animal resting from a night of prowling. Birds hawked and wheeled overhead and the only sign of life was a Mexican riding a burro, and he was over on the next street, leaving the town for the vastness of the land beyond.

She went to the side of the house and saw the pucker in the adobe where the stray bullet had struck, and when she looked by her door, in the dust, she saw several dark splotches, as though a man had bled as he passed her house.

The adobe across the vacant lot was silent, as though no one lived there at all. I'm alone, she thought. Alone in a dead, parched town in a dead, parched land.

3

THE WELL was behind the adobe, half-way between the house and the barn, and Eloise McCaffey had to draw all her water in a bucket and carry it to the house. The scrubbing had pretty near emptied the barrel kept inside, so she took the bucket and made several trips to the well, and on one of these she saw the splotches in the dust and stopped and looked at them and thought how similar they were to the ones passing her—she dropped the bucket and ran toward the small barn and half fearfully opened the door.

When she stepped inside she heard a pistol being cocked, then a man sighed with relief and said, "Over here." He did not speak loudly, but she turned and found him in one of the stalls, half-propped erect, blood staining the side of his shirt.

"Who—who're you? How did you get here?"

He grinned weakly. "Couldn't get much—farther." He was a young man with a thick shock of dark hair and steady blue eyes. "Fell off m'horse. Crawled here. Sorry."

"I'll go get help," she said and started to turn.

"No!" He shook his head. "I'm a dead man if Dan or Al Gannon find me."

"I'll be back," she said and went to the adobe. She got one of her good sheets and on the way back picked up the water bucket and filled it and then went on to the barn. He didn't want her to fuss over him, but she did anyway. His wound was ugly and he had lost a lot of blood, but she didn't think he'd die.

He told his name—Mike Shotten—and he let her bandage him tightly.

"I've never seen you before," Shotten said. "New to town?"

"Yes. My husband's in the army."

"An officer, I'll bet. The man who got you would have to be somebody. You've got class."

"Maybe you'd better not talk so much," Eloise said. "You can stay here until after dark. No one will see you leave then."

"Where would I go?" Shotten asked. "The Gannons would gun me down on sight. They put a price on my head. Two hundred dollars."

"Are you an outlaw?"

"I am if you ask Dan Gannon anything, or one of his friends." He looked steadily at her. "You'd be two hundred dollars richer if you yelled for help."

"I don't need two hundred dollars," she said firmly. "You stay here until my husband gets back. Maybe tomorrow or the next day. When it gets dark, I'll bring you something to eat. Until then you'll have to put up with being hungry."

"How come you're doing this for me?"

"Because Dan Gannon is a lout," she said and went back to the adobe. Then she started to think about Mike Shotten; if his situation was so desperate it was likely that the Gannon brothers would try to pick up his trail, and it was pretty plain in her back yard.

After thinking about it, she got out the tub and all the dirty clothes she could find and took them out back and started to wash, and in no time at all she had spilled enough to make a muddy mess of any sign Mike Shotten had left getting to the barn.

And none too soon for Dan and Al Gannon rode past, followed by four mounted men, and they examined the road carefully before coming around behind the adobe where Eloise worked.

Dan Gannon smiled handsomely. "Mornin' there. I guess you heard shootin' last night."

"Do I look deaf?" She looked at the men with Gannon. "Yes, I heard it. What of it?"

"I don't suppose you saw anyone around here?"

"No I didn't." One man crowded his horse close to her and she glared at him. "Back up. What do you think you're doing?"

"Lookin'," he said, grinning.

"Look someplace else," she warned, and when he took no heed, she slapped the horse across the head with a wet sheet and immediately set the animal to violent pitching. The rider clung to his seat, but the horse broke into a wild run and both the Gannons laughed.

"Ain't you the feisty one," Dan Gannon said. "Come on, there's nothin' for us here. Leastways, not what we came after." They rode out, raising a rank cloud of dust, and the washing she had on the line had to be done over.

With the work started, she finished it, then changed her dress and went to the center of town. She left her order with Twilling at the store, to be delivered later, then went in search of the sheriff's office. She found it, a small place crowded between the feed store and the assay office, and she opened the door.

Dan Gannon took his feet off the desk and smiled. "I knew you'd come to me sooner or later, but I didn't reckon it would be so quick."

"You? The sheriff?"

"Yep. I don't wear a badge 'cause everyone knows me. What can I do for you, honey?"

"You can stop getting smart with me," Eloise said. "The first thing my husband's going to do when he gets back is to knock you down."

Gannon grinned. "Want to bet?"

"What do you mean?"

"I hear that he's going to build up old Camp Grant. To do that he'll need men. I've got the men and they don't turn a lick without my say-so. Sure, I guess he'll look me up as soon as he comes back to Tucson, but it won't be to knock me down, even if he could."

She stared at him. "What makes you so despicable?"

"What's that mean? I come by my good looks naturally." He grinned and straightened his tie.

"I wasn't flattering you, Mr. Gannon. Not at all."

"Didn't think you was," he said, his humor fading.

"Tucson ain't much, the way you see it. It's different for me. Maybe it's because this is my town, and the bigger it gets, the bigger I get. Someday I'm going to own it all, or all that's worth ownin', and when a man wants anything done, he'll ask me first, and say, please, Mr. Gannon."

"My," she said, "we're filled with a fool's ambitions, aren't we?"

"You might think so," he said, "but you'd be wrong. All that's holding up progress now is the Apaches. There's gold here, and cattle country, but it'll take a strong man to open it up. I got the army in here." He tapped himself on the chest with his finger. "I played politics and bought whiskey and made love to the senators' wives in Washington and danced with their clumsy daughters, but I got it going, a move to drive the Apaches back and open up this country."

"What is this going to cost, Mr. Gannon? In soldiers' lives, and Apache lives?"

"Who cares? The soldiers they scrape out of the gutters of Baltimore and Chicago and New Orleans. The Apaches?" He shrugged. "I don't care about the Apaches."

"There's a hint of a drawl in your voice. Were you in the Confederacy?"

He shook his head. "I don't fight for the losing side of anything. No, I sold what I had and came here in '61."

"I see. Mr. Gannon, you were making quite a fuss this morning, hunting down a man. Was that a posse with you?"

"Some friends that help out now and then," he said. "The man I want tried to kill me last night, but he was driven off." He came around the desk and stood near her, yet she showed no fear of him. "It's not your business so I won't bother you with it." He opened the door for her and stood there, smiling. "I'm not even going to ask you what you wanted with the sheriff, because I'll find out sooner or later."

"Yes, you're very clever," she said and went on down the street. She had an excuse to stop in Twilling's store, and did so. Business was slack and she went to the counter. "Mr. Twilling, who's Mike Shotten?"

"A man mighty handy with his pistol," Twilling said.

She explained that Gannon and his men had been searching for Shotten and Twilling nodded. "So that's what the shootin' was last night. Woke me from a sound sleep. They didn't get Shotten, so I guess it ain't ended yet."

"What isn't ended?"

"The war goin' on between Gannon and Shotten," he said. "When Mike got out of the army, he came here and Gannon put him to work, sellin' whiskey to the Apaches mostly. Somehow this went agin' Shotten's grain and he backed away from Gannon. A man just don't do that, you know. Rumor has it that Shotten found him an Injun woman and took up with her, but I never believed it; he's a clean-livin' kind of fella. Don't cuss, don't drink, never seen him smoke or speak anything but polite to a lady. Anyway, him and Gannon pulled pistols on each other some time back. It was a real free for all, them runnin' around the streets, bangin' away at each other. Finally some of Gannon's friends showed up and it got too hot for Shotten, and he left. Lives in the hills and is mighty careful where he shows himself. This is Gannon country and there ain't anythin' goin' to change that."

"Do you really believe that? Never mind. Is Mr. Shotten a criminal?"

Twilling scratched his head. "Gannon says he is and he's the law, but it was Gannon's laws that got broke, not anyone else's. No, I'd say he was no worse, no better than anyone else."

"Thank you," she said and started for the door.

He hurried around the counter to catch up with her. "Why all the interest in Mike Shotten?"

"I am interested in anything or anyone who sets himself against Dan Gannon," she said. "Does that answer your question?"

"Reckon it does," he said, smiling. "You've got company but they won't come out and say it like you do."

"You, Mr. Twilling?"

"Well, I've had my nose pinched and didn't like it." He

nodded. "I'd work against Gannon, long as I wasn't caught. I ain't brave, you know."

"Is there a doctor in town?"

"There's one that says he is. No one's ever argued about it, 'cause he's saved a few and had a few die on him. Why?"

"Send him to me after dark," she said. "And have him take care not to be seen."

"Say—" He held out his hand but she had swept out and was walking down the street.

She did not go near the barn and when the sun went down, she left her front door open and cleared away the supper dishes. Finally she heard a step, and a small, whisk-ered man paused before knocking.

"Hello. I'm Dr. Caswell. Twilling told me—"

"Come in," she said. "Sit down. The place is a mess but I've just moved in and—"

"People only call me when there's a mess," Caswell said and wiped his glasses. "You don't look sick? Pregnant?"

"Neither," Eloise said. "Doctor, are you afraid of Dan Gannon?"

"No more than the next man, which is considerable," he said frankly. "What's Gannon got to do with my being here?"

"He's after Mike Shotten."

Caswell shrugged. "He's been after Mike for nearly a year, but he ain't caught him yet, and if I know Dan, he's hoping he won't catch him while he's alone."

"You heard about the shooting last night?"

"I heard there was some shooting," Caswell said. He studied her carefully. "Where is Shotten?"

"In the barn," she said. "Come along." She picked up the lamp, blew it out, and led the way to the back.

Once inside, she put a match to the wick and looked into the stall. Mike Shotten had his pistol leveled at Doctor Caswell, then let it sag. "Howdy, Fred. Sorry I can't get up."

Caswell glanced at Eloise McCaffey, then quickly knelt and unwrapped the bandage around Shotten's waist. He examined the wound, especially the exit hole, then started to re-bandage it.

A horseman riding up to the adobe alerted them and Eloise quickly put out the lamp. Caswell came to the door with her and looked out as the horseman came on to the barn. Then Eloise gave a glad cry and said, "It's my husband. Linus, in here." Caswell relit the lamp as McCaffey dismounted and came in, flogging dust from his clothes.

He looked around, saw Shotten and Caswell, and then he said, "I'll bet someone can explain this."

"This is Mike Shotten," Eloise said. "And Doctor Caswell. Mr. Shotten has been hiding in the barn since late last night." She smiled at him and was a little puzzled to see him frowning.

"Everything is perfectly clear to me," McCaffey said, stripping off his gauntlets. He walked over and stood near Shotten, looking down at him. "You were cleaning your gun and it went off."

"Your wife is a gallant woman, sir," Shotten said. "I owe her my life."

"My wife is a quick-tempered, dunderheaded Irish woman who is full of surprises. Doctor, let's get this man into the house."

"No, you don't understand," Eloise said. "Dan Gannon is trying to kill him."

Linus McCaffey smiled. "I don't know any Dan Gannon, and if I did, it wouldn't bother me one way or another. No one is going to be killed in my house, so if you'll take one side, doctor, I'll take the other."

"Most gallant of you, sir," Shotten said as they helped him stand. Pain bit at him but he made no cry and they carefully took him into the adobe. He protested when they put him on the bed.

Doctor Caswell said, "You'll be more comfortable here, Mike, but you know that Gannon will find out you're here."

"It's inevitable, I suppose," Shotten said. He looked at Linus McCaffey. "You're obviously a brave man, sir, but impetuous. I'd best leave soon."

"This is my house, and you're a guest. If this Gannon

wants a hole put in his head, let him come and start something."

"Oh, he'll come," Caswell said, picking up his bag. "You'll learn that he's reliable, in some things."

4

"MR. SHOTTEN is an outlaw," Eloise said sweetly. "To hear Mr. Gannon tell it."

"I see," Linus McCaffey said. He took off his blouse and rolled the sleeves of his underwear and washed his hands and face. Then he turned and looked at Mike Shotten. "I trust your crime was to look crossways at this fellow, Gannon, or something equally severe."

Shotten smiled. "That's crime enough in this part of the territory."

Eloise poked up a fire and put on some coffee. "Linus, you already met Al Gannon."

He turned to her in surprise. "I have?"

"Yes, you knocked him down for smoking cigars on the stage."

He chuckled. "Well now, this is taking on some elements of pleasure." He explained the incident to Shotten, who was highly amused by it.

"Dan would have been a little harder to handle," Shotten said. "But you'll get your chance to find that out."

"I'll be looking forward to it," McCaffey said. He got cups and poured the coffee, then sat at the table and stretched out his legs. "I suppose I arrived here in a sour frame of mind concerning Dan Gannon. The name was beginning to irritate my ears for all Captain Lovering could seem to say was Dan Gannon this and Dan Gannon that. If I wanted wagons and teamsters, I'd have to see Dan Gannon. For labor, see Dan Gannon. Damn it, you'd think a man had to ask Dan Gannon for permission to spit."

"That's not far off," Shotten said. "The man came here

when there wasn't much. It would be near the truth to say that he built the town to what it is, and he'll go on building. Dan took some big risks and naturally figured they entitle him to a lot of say."

"What does the brother—Al? Is that his name? What does he do?"

"He thinks," Shotten said. "Dan does, but Al thinks of what he'll do."

McCaffey took out his watch and looked at it. "For a man of action, Gannon is taking his time about getting here. Of course, I don't suppose the doctor ran and told him you were here."

"No," Shotten said, "he wouldn't do that. A lot of people are against Dan, but few men want to stand up to him." He looked at Eloise. "Could I trouble you to go to the barn for my bullet pouch and powder flask? I may have need of them."

"Is your cylinder fully charged?" McCaffey asked.

Shotten nodded.

"Then I think we're well enough armed," McCaffey said. "I see your pistol is a Remington. So is mine. If it comes to that, I'll share some ammunition with you." He looked at his watch again. "No doubt by now one of Gannon's men has reported that the doctor came to this house. He will draw the correct conclusion, I'm sure." He got up and poured some more coffee and Mike Shotten watched him.

"You're a calm man, Mr. McCaffey; I admire that."

"Pretty senseless to become excited," he said.

Finally he heard what he was listening for, a man's step outside, and the low, soft voice of one man speaking to another. Then the door rattled beneath hard knuckles.

"Who is it?" McCaffey asked. He got up and slipped his cap and ball pistol from the holster.

"Dan Gannon. Open the door."

McCaffey slid the bolt and Gannon pushed the door open, but he only put one foot over the threshold for McCaffey put the muzzle of the .44 against his stomach and cocked it.

Gannon looked at the gun, then at McCaffey. "You're not very friendly at all."

"That is true," McCaffey said. "You want in? Come in." He grabbed Gannon by the thick shock of hair and jerked him into the room, at the same time tripping him with an outstretched foot and sending him sprawling. One of his pearl-handled pistols slid from the holster and he reached for the other one.

McCaffey kicked out and caught him on the wrist, making Gannon yelp in sudden pain. Outside, a man yelled, "Dan? Dan, you all right in there?"

"Reply wisely," McCaffey said and bent to disarm Gannon.

"It's all right!" Gannon yelled. He looked at McCaffey from his position on the floor. "You won't do anything to me, lieutenant. I've got men outside." He got to his feet and brushed off his clothes.

Eloise said, "Now you've insulted me. I scrubbed this place clean."

"Close the door, dear, and pick up Mr. Gannon's pistols. He strikes me as a man who would do something stupidly fatal just to show us how brave he is." He sat down at the table and laid his pistol to one side. "Scoot a chair around, Mr. Gannon. Over that way a bit. Now if you'll glance over your shoulder, you'll see that Mr. Shotten has his revolver pretty much centered on your spine. I hope it doesn't make you nervous. He seems to have a steady hand."

"Al said you were a cool one," Gannon said. He smiled and took a cigar from his pocket. "Do you mind if I smoke? You seem to have a dislike for cigars."

"Rather the men who now and then smoke them," McCaffey said. "I'm sorry you're going to be disappointed, but you're not going to get Shotten this time."

"Kind of looks that way, doesn't it?" He shrugged. "I can wait, although I don't like to." He turned his head and looked at Mike Shotten. "You've got the devil's luck if I ever saw it."

"Tell me something," McCaffey asked. "Did you really expect to take Shotten from me?"

"You can't keep him here very long," Gannon said. "I want him, McCaffey, and I'll get him. If I can't have him tonight, then I'll get him when he leaves. Let's see you stop that."

Al Gannon began to pound on the door, calling for his brother, and McCaffey picked up his pistol, but Dan Gannon shouted before he could send a bullet through the door.

"Go on home! There's nothing doing tonight!"

"Are you sure, Dan? I can get some men and—"

"Go on home! I'll see you later!"

Al Gannon turned away from the door and McCaffey put his pistol down. Eloise McCaffey tapped Dan Gannon on the shoulder and said, "You haven't called me honey once this evening. Am I losing my allure or something?"

McCaffey's glance sharpened. "What's this?"

"Mr. Gannon considers himself irresistible to women," Eloise said frankly. "He's been entertaining ideas. Haven't you, Mr. Gannon?"

Mike Shotten laughed. "Bein' the ladies' man is catchin' up with you, Dan."

"Aw, shut your mouth," Gannon said sourly.

Linus McCaffey got up and put his pistol in the holster and unbuckled the flap before removing the belt and tossing it to Shotten on the bed. Then when he kicked his chair back out of the way, Dan Gannon smiled and got up.

"I'm going to like this," he said and swung.

McCaffey let it "whump" off his shoulder and he jabbed out with his left, the fist moving like the bearing journal on a locomotive driver, just going so far, then stopping. But it was far enough to hit Gannon flush in the mouth, making his head snap back. His hat flew off and his hair jumped, and tears dampened his eyes from the sting of it.

McCaffey could have hit Gannon again in that moment, but he passed it up and danced away from the table, making Gannon bring the fight to him.

Gannon's style was rough and blunt and manly; he

charged McCaffey, swung and fanned the air for McCaffey was quick on his feet and he knew how to duck a punch. And he had style, learned the hard way in the Academy gymnasium; he kept flicking out his left hand, jolting Gannon, making angry red welts on his cheekbones, and bruising his nose and eyebrows and mouth.

The anger was beginning to take hold of Gannon, the frustration a man can know when he desires desperately to hurt another yet can't seem to bring it about. He had not landed one solid punch on McCaffey's face although he had hit him in the body several times, which could hurt a man more than a head blow. But it wasn't what Gannon wanted. He wanted the blood showing on McCaffey's face and he just couldn't reach him.

Shotten said, "Dan, he's going to cut you to pieces."

It enraged Gannon, to hear the truth flung at him by his enemy and before either man could prepare for it, he wheeled, bounded across the room, and struck Shotten as he lay on the bed.

Eloise gasped, then said, "You'll never be able to think of yourself as a brave, noble man again, Mr. Gannon."

He stood there, panting, looking at McCaffey and his wife, and looking at his pair of pearl-handled revolvers laying on the table by the wooden sink.

"You'll never make them," McCaffey said. "I'm here, Gannon. Waiting. Come to me, man. If there is any man in you. Come to me or crawl away. Take your choice."

"I can lick you," Gannon said and sprang for McCaffey. He came as an angry man comes, without caution, convinced by his own rage that he would sweep aside any obstacle and crush his enemy.

McCaffey kited a chair directly into Gannon's path, tangling the man's legs, crashing him to the floor. He kicked away from the broken chair and staggered erect, bleeding from the nose.

"Now I'll take it to you," McCaffey said and went into him.

He clipped away with his left, hitting Gannon with annoying regularity, blocking Gannon's looping blows, letting them bounce off his shoulders and arms. He brought blood down into Gannon's eyes so that he had to keep raising his hands to wipe them clear enough to see.

McCaffey hit him then with his right hand, for the first time and Gannon crashed back against the wall. He started to stagger clear of it, but McCaffey wouldn't have it. He gripped Gannon by the throat and weathered the man's failing punches and kept cutting and chopping at him with his right hand. Gannon's vision was gone and he bubbled through his nose, and finally McCaffey let him go and Gannon simply sagged to a sitting position and stayed there, mumbling sadly to himself.

Shotten said soberly, "He don't even know where he is now."

McCaffey went to the sink board and got both of Gannon's pistols and jammed them deep in the man's holsters. "Find me a board and some string and something to write with," he said, glancing at his wife.

She got a piece of a packing box and he wrote with the soot from the bottom of the coffee pot and then he fastened string to the board and hung it around Gannon's neck.

Eloise said, "What are you going to do, Linus?"

"Take him uptown where they can look at him."

She looked at the sign. "That's hard, Linus."

"He's got to learn."

Shotten said, "Take my pistol and belt. There's no flap on it and you may need a weapon in a hurry."

"I'll do it my way," McCaffey said. He got Gannon to his feet, for the man was conscious, but unable to see, and he unbolted the door and took him outside and steered him toward the center of town.

The busiest place was the saloon, and McCaffey marched him unsteadily down the street and Gannon kept saying, "I'll kill you. I'll kill you," and McCaffey paid no attention to him at all.

The laughter and guitar playing stopped abruptly when McCaffey pushed him through the door and gave him a shove into the room. Gannon blindly fell against a table and braced himself there, arms stiff, looking from side to side, but seeing nothing through the puffed eye-lids.

One man said, "Say, ain't that Dan Gannon? You can't hardly tell." He walked over to Gannon and looked at the sign. "What's that say, Pete? I don't read too good."

"You don't read at all," the bartender said. He read aloud. "*I MOLEST DECENT WOMEN.*" He swallowed hard and Gannon struck the table with his fist. He looked at McCaffey and saw some discoloring on his face. "You do this, lieutenant?" He didn't wait for his answer. "Couple of you fellas give Dan a hand there. Sit him down. Willie, get him a drink." He reached for the sign, meaning to take it off.

"Leave it there!" McCaffey said flatly and everyone looked at him. "Every dog ought to wear a collar."

The bartender said, "You've gone too far."

"No, he went too far," McCaffey said. "Anyone want to argue the point?"

"You can't do this kind of thing to a man," someone said.

"I didn't do it to a *man*," McCaffey said and walked out of the place.

Eloise was waiting in the doorway when he came back and he took off his pistol belt and threw it on the table. "I could use a drink," he said. "But unfortunately I'm a teetotaler." He blew out a long breath and looked at his wife. "You saw a side of me that I'd liked to have kept hidden, Eloise. Can you forget it?"

"No, but I never thought you were a jackrabbit, Linus. If a woman has to choose, she'll take a hard man over a weak one." She patted his arm. "I've made some more coffee. I'll get you some. You too, Mr. Shotten?"

"I would, thanks." He smiled. "And if I don't run any risks of running into Dan Gannon's trouble, you could call me Mike." He offered McCaffey his hand. "I don't do this, as a rule, because it's been a long time since I met a man Gannon couldn't scare. Maybe we could work together."

"I've already got my job cut out for me," McCaffey

said. "Gannon's going to make it tough too. Or impossible."

"That's why I say we ought to work together," Shotten said, accepting the coffee Eloise brought to him. "Gannon may have everyone under his thumb around here, but given thirty days, I could get you a hundred men who'd work no matter what Gannon said. Not from around here though."

"I'd be happy with fifty men," McCaffey said. "Captain Lovering wants me to start building right away."

"How'll you pay?" Shotten asked.

"Gold. Twice a month."

Shotten grinned. "You just help me get out of Tucson alive and I'll get your men."

"All right," McCaffey said. "Say, I never asked, but what were you doing here anyway if you knew Gannon was after you?"

Shotten glanced at Eloise, then said, "I got lonely for company, I guess. It's a weakness some men have."

"That doesn't make sense," McCaffey said, rising.

"To some it don't," Shotten said and drank his coffee.

5

When Lieutenant McCaffey failed to report for duty, Captain Lovering became quite upset and irritated, and he sent Private Noonan to town to see what was keeping McCaffey. Then Noonan came back with his report.

"Sir, there's a ring of fellas around the lootenant's house. They wouldn't let me in to talk to him."

"That's ridiculous," Lovering said.

"Yes, sir. They wouldn't let the lootenant out either. I thought it was best to come and tell you, sir."

"All right, Noonan. Send Sergeant Baker here and wait outside." He drummed his fingers on the desk until the sergeant came in, a short, blocky man with a heavy face and a constant scowl etched there by twenty years of handling balky recruits.

"You send for me, sir?"

"Yes," Lovering said. "Noonan reports that Lieutenant McCaffey is unable to leave his house; he seems to be besieged by a group of civilians. Form a five-man detail and we'll go into Tucson and look into this. Take Noonan along."

"Do I have to, sir?" When Lovering's glance came up, Baker swallowed. "Yes, sir. Noonan it is." He saluted and went out and Lovering worked on a report until Baker had the detail ready to mount up. Then Lovering took up his pistol belt and buckled it as he went out.

He was a no-nonsense man on the march and made a short trip of it. As he led his detail down the narrow street to McCaffey's adobe, he saw the men leaning against the opposite walls. Two were standing in the vacant lot between McCaffey's and Bessie's place, and he imagined another stood in the alley behind McCaffey's barn.

Al Gannon came across the street to meet Lovering, and the detail was halted.

"What's going on here?" Lovering asked.

"A little private business," Gannon said. He took off his derby and wiped away sweat trapped on his forehead. "You want to mess in it, captain?"

Lovering looked steadily at him for a moment, then gave the order without taking his eyes off Gannon. "Ready carbines, sergeant. Forward. Shoot the first man who makes a move." He nudged his horse into motion and Al Gannon had to quickly step aside or be run down.

The man who had been standing across the street with Gannon stepped away from the wall, and Lovering spoke to Baker. "Cover me, sergeant."

The detail halted and the troopers wheeled their horses and faced outward, carbine butts on their thighs, waiting for Al Gannon to make the next move. Without hesitation, Paul Lovering dismounted in front of McCaffey's adobe and went to the door. It opened before he reached it and McCaffey said, "I knew when they sent Noonan back that you'd come in, sir."

"What kind of a mess have we here?" Lovering asked.

"Come in," McCaffey said and stepped back. He left the door open.

Lovering saw Mike Shotten sitting on the edge of the bed. He frowned and said, "I might have known you'd be mixed up in this, Shotten. Now I know who Al Gannon is after. Where's Dan?"

"Under the weather," Shotten said. "Linus had an argument with him last night. Dan's not quite able to make it to his feet."

"I see," Lovering said. "All right, let's get out of here. We can't hold up army business because the Gannons don't like it. Can you navigate all right, Shotten?"

"With some help. I'll need a horse."

"Better make that a wagon, captain," McCaffey said. "He might open that wound again."

Lovering thought about it, then nodded. "I'll get Baker on it." He went to the door and signaled for the sergeant to come over. Quickly he explained what he wanted and after Baker left, Al Gannon approached the door.

He said, "Captain, we ought to be able to do some horse tradin' here."

"What have you got to trade?"

Gannon felt that he was on firmer ground now. "The bone I've got to pick with the lieutenant here can wait until Dan is up and around. But him," he pointed to Mike Shotten— "he's an outlaw and I want him. No ifs ands or buts about it."

"Do you have a warrant for his arrest?"

"Don't need one," Al Gannon said. "Dan's the sheriff and he says Mike's an outlaw. That's good enough for me."

"And who says that your brother is the law?" Lovering asked.

Gannon was beginning to grow irritated. "Damn it, he says so. There wasn't no law at all until he took over. Now I want Shotten."

"You can't have him," McCaffey said. "He's already under arrest and in military custody."

Lovering's eyebrow went up for he didn't quite see what McCaffey was getting at, but Al Gannon showed an outright anger. "On what charge? You tell me that."

"Loitering in my barn," McCaffey said.

Gannon snorted in disgust and laughed at the same time. "Why, that's ridiculous! There's no such a law."

"Yes there is, because I made it up. Just the way your brother made up his own authority. Captain, will you honor this arrest?"

"Certainly," Lovering said, his manner growing brisk. "This throws a different complexion on the problem, Gannon. Since this is now entirely military business, I'm ordering your men to clear out. If there is any step taken to block me, my troops will fire." He poked his finger at Al Gannon. "And get this clear: you are dealing with the United States Government now. To make a wrong move would be most disastrous to you." He saw that Baker was returning with a team and wagon. "I'm afraid, Mr. Gannon, that this matter will have to terminate here, and the question of legality will be settled in a court of law."

"Aw, to hell with it," Al muttered. "There'll be another day." He spun on his heel and walked to the street, signaling for his men to join him. Then they walked on toward the center of town.

Paul Lovering said, "I don't think we'll ever have a clearer path. Sergeant, will you give Mr. Shotten a hand into the wagon? Thank you." He turned to Eloise McCaffey. "You've had quite a bit of excitement here. Would you feel safer back on the post? We'll crowd you in somewhere."

"I'll stay here until Linus sends for me," she said. "I'm really not afraid."

"She's telling you the truth," McCaffey said, smiling. He put his arm around her. "When she was eight she could lick any boy on the block. The first thing I noticed about her was her solid right to the jaw."

"Isn't that sweet?" Eloise said. She kissed him. "Now go on. You're holding up the United States Army."

Lovering said, "Pardon me for bringing this up, Mr. McCaffey, but that kiss will have to last you for sixty days. I want you to ride out with the preliminary survey party this afternoon." He looked from one to the other, then added, "I think I'll look to my horse. We'll return to the post in five minutes."

He stepped out and Linus McCaffey shrugged. "You heard the captain. Sixty days? I'll write and send it on with the dispatch rider. But don't worry, it's only temporary."

"I won't worry, but I'll be impatient for you to get back," she said. "Linus, do you think we ought to get a family started?"

"Ah—not for sixty days anyway," he said and kissed

her again before leaving. A trooper had saddled his horse and brought it around from the barn.

Lovering ordered them to mount, then started out, and he drove through the center of town, the troopers flanking the wagon, with one bringing up the rear, for he wanted the town to see what had been taken away from Dan Gannon, a feat not often viewed in Tucson.

At the post, the surgeon looked at Shotten's wound and declared that it was healing nicely; he would be able to ride in a week, if he didn't run the horse.

McCaffey shared the noon meal with Captain Lovering, at his quarters, and afterward they went to headquarters to discuss Mike Shotten's offer for help.

"There's no denying the man has a power in some parts of the territory," Lovering said. "He'll provide Mexican labor, of course, but I don't suppose you'll have any more trouble from them than you would the riffraff Dan Gannon would supply. I'm giving you eight men, Mr. McCaffey. Sergeant Baker is a good surveyor, as well as an excellent line sergeant. One man to cook, four to maintain guard and two to handle the odd jobs and spell the guards. How you deploy them is your own affair. However, it would please me to report in sixty days that you had the site surveyed and markers up so that construction can begin."

"The schedule seems most flexible," McCaffey said.

"Yes, it does seem that way, but you'll likely have problems. The Apaches may visit you, to look you over, or to fight; only an Apache seems able to decide which that will be. Your force will be small, but heavily armed, which is something the Apaches always respect. I've issued orders that each man will have two sidearms, forty rounds apiece, a carbine, and three spares, with a hundred and fifty rounds for each. Pack mules will transport the rest of the gear, tents, food supplies, tools, and some Vulcan powder for blasting. You can use Noonan as a dispatch rider. In spite of his bottle tippling, he knows the country and he's a fighter." He smiled. "Somehow, Linus, you've earned the man's respect. It's a good sign, for he seemed to have lost his own some time ago."

There were a few other things to discuss, and by the time they were settled, the detail was making up to leave the post. McCaffey was given maps, but he left them in his dispatch case, for he didn't want to have the men under him think he couldn't remember the way, having been to the site once before. An enlisted man picked on these little details in an officer, and unless they trusted him completely, they wouldn't be inclined to accept his orders blindly.

McCaffey had his choice, to make a straight through march of it to show how tough he could be, or to make a late night camp and arrive late the next day. He decided on the latter, giving the men some rest and saving the animals. Some might put him down as soft for doing this, while others might regard it as considerate, and he believed they would take this view over the other.

Noonan came around and squatted down. "S'cuse me, sir, but I hear you gave Dan Gannon a hell of a beating."

"There was some battering back and forth," McCaffey said.

"Did you really close both his eyes?"

"He couldn't see very well, that's true," McCaffey said and wished that Noonan would talk about something else. Then he began to think that Noonan *had* to talk about it.

"And the sign?"

"You know what it said," McCaffey said. "Noonan, what's your point?"

"Nothin'," the man said, but he sounded relieved. Happy and relieved.

"You're not honest with me, soldier. What have you got against Gannon?"

"Everything," Noonan said. "Lootenant, I had a wife. He made goo-goo eyes at her while I was out and she left me for him."

"I see."

"No, you don't see. Lootenant, he left her in a whorehouse. That's what he did. I found her in Yuma and she took acid and killed herself rather than come back to me." He rolled up his sleeves and showed Gannon his arms and the firelight threw shadows against the lumps caused by poorly-healed fractures. "I went after him and he did this to me with his boots after I was down on the ground and out cold. Both arms broke, lootenant. Yeah, I got everything against Dan Gannon, but it's been evened a little now."

"Noonan, I'm sorry. Sorry as hell," McCaffey said.

"I know you are," he said. "Yes, sir, I really know that. Some men can say they're sorry and they ain't a damned bit, but I know you're really sorry." He hesitated and wiped a hand across his face. "Lootenant, I really didn't have anything against you."

"I know that, Noonan." Then he said, very gently, "Are you figuring on killing him someday?"

Noonan thought a bit. "I guess so. Maybe I can give up the bottle then and start livin' like a man again." He shrugged. "But if I did, he'd just be dead and my Rosie'd still be dead and nothing' would be changed at all."

"We've got a job to do," McCaffey said. "We're army, Noonan; I don't ever want you to forget that."

"Yes, sir."

"Now go to your blankets and get some sleep."

The man left and McCaffey settled back. Sergeant Baker came over and spoke softly. "If he gives you trouble, Lieutenant—"

"It's rather the other way around," McCaffey said. "Do you know about Noonan's troubles?"

"Second hand," Baker said. "Meanin' no disrespect, but we always knew that Dan would roll his eyes at the wrong man's woman. There ain't a married man on the post who don't owe you for what you did."

McCaffey raised up on an elbow. "Well, things certainly get around out here, don't they?"

Baker grinned, and it was like a brown boot top folding into a myriad of small wrinkles. "Yes, sir. We know what's going on. And right off you've moved to the top bull of this here lick."

"A dubious honor, to be sure," McCaffey said.

Baker shook his head. "Now don't figure it wrong, sir. A man's got to be some man out here or he won't get anyplace."

6

THE SITE chosen to build the post was the junction of the Aravaypa and the San Pedro rivers, both at a low ebb, and as soon as the full heat of summer came, they would be as dry as the sutler's cracker barrel.

Three buildings stood on the site, all adobe, the remains of an old trading post, and from this meager beginning, McCaffey meant to build something fit for military occupancy. The post would be rectangular, the four sides being rows of officers' quarters, the adjutant's office, the post bakery, the guardhouse near the entrance, the commissary and quartermaster stores to the south. And behind all this, like an appendage, would be the blacksmith's shops, the corrals, the stables, and the enlisted men's quarters.

With hand tools and two weeks of hard labor, McCaffey and his detail cleared the site of brush and rock. With Baker on the "stick," McCaffey surveyed the perimeter and drove his stakes.

Several times during their work they saw Apaches, but always at a distance, and every man worked heavily armed, which in Baker's opinion, kept the Apaches at bay.

Unable to start new construction without workers, McCaffey turned his attention to repairing the existing buildings. Time and weather had all but ruined the roof structure, and McCaffey had his detail cutting saplings and plastering mud, and he was finishing this chore when Baker called to him, and pointed.

Four Apaches were approaching; they were still several hundred yards away. Baker came over to McCaffey and said, "We hadn't ought to let 'em get too close, sir."

"I see only one rifle among them," he said. He looked around. "Anyone speak Apache?"

No one did, and McCaffey supposed that the Apaches would speak no English. "A fine thing," he said.

Baker looked at him. "What is?"

"Nothing," he said. "Just thinking out loud."

Two of the Apaches stopped and sat down while the other two came on. They were near-naked, dirty people, armed with bows and arrows, and knives dangling from a thong around their waists.

The spokesman was tall and well-muscled, a man of thirty, bold-faced and apparently fearless. He talked and none of it made sense to McCaffey, and even when he pointed to the soldiers and the buildings, it only confused the young officer. Whether the Apache liked or disliked the idea was beyond him.

Baker said, "You ought to answer him, sir."

"He wouldn't understand it if I did," McCaffey said.

"Yes, but it would be talk. I think he'll be a little insulted if you don't address some remarks to him."

"Very well," McCaffey said. He looked at the Indian. "Go to hell."

The Apache began a new, more voluble argument and concluded it by shooting one of his arrows into the ground at McCaffey's feet.

McCaffey looked at it a moment, then swept his foot out and broke it cleanly. The Apache gave a roar of rage and snatched his knife from his belt and swiped at McCaffey, who barely had time to pull back. Even then the bare tip of the knife ripped his blouse cleanly across without touching his flesh.

Baker, recovering from his surprise, swung his carbine and knocked the knife out of the Apache's hand. It fell in the dirt and he lunged for it, but McCaffey stamped his foot down on it and looked at the Apache.

"I think this man wants to fight, sergeant." He ripped off his ruined blouse and flung it aside and the Apache stepped back to wait.

"Better watch out, sir. These fellas are good wrestlers. He'll gouge your eyes out, or bite your ear off if he gets a chance."

"I'm sure he would," McCaffey said. "Step back, sergeant." He kicked the knife completely out of reach, then knocked the Indian flat on his back with one punch.

He hadn't meant to knock the Apache out and he didn't, but he hurt him a little and showed him clearly that he could be hurt.

The Indian knew nothing of fist fighting, but he was a wrestler, and as quick as a cat. When McCaffey flicked his left out again, the Indian grabbed the wrist, whirled and threw McCaffey over his shoulder.

The ground was sandy, which eased the fall, but still it jarred McCaffey and before he could even roll over, the Apache was on him, twisting his arm painfully behind him. He's going to break it, McCaffey thought, and with his free hand he managed to reach back and poke the Apache in the eye, making him release the grip.

McCaffey got up, wringing his pained arm, restoring some circulation to it. He dodged a kick, then hit the Apache in the mouth, knocking him back, and he went after him, a mistake if he ever made one for the Apache grabbed him, fell back, and with a foot in McCaffey's stomach, again sailed him through the air.

This time, McCaffey rolled as he hit, and none too soon for the Apache bombed dust as he crashed into the ground, intending to fall on top of McCaffey.

"Tricky bastard," McCaffey said and got to his feet.

He circled the Apache like a weasel sizing up a spring layer, and he kept darting out his hand, not touching the Apache, but getting him into the habit of ducking to the left. Then when he had him set up nicely, he feigned with the left, uncorked the right, and put him into the happy hunting ground with one blow.

The Apache hit like a tossed sack of meal, and he lay perfectly still, his jaw slightly askew for it was badly fractured. From the two Apaches who waited some distance away, a moan went up, and McCaffey turned his back on the downed man and went over to the water bucket to splash some over his face.

"Get them on their way, sergeant," he said and Baker shooed them from camp. The beaten man had to be carried and they took him some distance away, then the Apache with the rifle fired and one of the troopers swore as the ball nicked his arm.

McCaffey wheeled and almost gave the order to fire, but he held it back, thinking that the beaten man must have been some kind of champion to their people and he couldn't blame them for expressing anger.

The trooper was barely scratched and once the wound was bandaged, everyone forgot about it. McCaffey was beginning to feel a little stiffness in his muscles for he had hit harder than he realized.

When Baker came over, he said, "You were right, sergeant. They can wrestle." Then he smiled. "I believe the Academy wrestling coach could take a lesson or two from that man."

"It's one of their favorite sports," Baker said.

McCaffey raised an eyebrow. "Sport? Good Lord, I'm leaving before the war starts." He shook his head. "Too bad we couldn't understand each other. Doesn't anyone around here speak Apache? Anyone on the post?"

"No, sir. I've never heard of a white man who could speak Apache. We don't know too much about 'em, sir, except that they like to kill any white man they find who ain't too well armed and who don't keep a sharp eye out to what he's doin'."

"What's the population of these Indians?"

Baker shrugged. "Don't know, sir. The thing is, you never see more than four or five together, and generally you don't see 'em at all. An arrow just whizzes out of nowhere and someone gets killed."

"Sounds like a rough kind of war, if you can call it war."

"Ain't much else you can call it," Baker said.

That evening, Mike Shotten rode into the camp and dismounted. "Six wagons and thirty men are less than four miles behind me. Maybe you could have coffee ready for them."

"We'll do better than that," McCaffey said. "Sergeant, tell the cook to put something together. He's got an hour." He offered Shotten a folding camp stool. "Sit down. Did you push straight through from Tucson?"

Shotten shook his head. "Never went near the place. No, we've been on the trail for six days. This is Thursday, isn't it? I lose track."

"Friday," McCaffey said. He told Shotten about the visit from the Apaches, and the fight, and Shotten listened very carefully.

"Describe this Apache to me."

"Tall, nearly six foot. A nice looking man in a savage way. Very intelligent eyes, and absolutely fearless."

"That was the one they call Cochise," Shotten said. "He's pretty much of a leader with his people. You really hurt him, huh?"

"Yes, I'm sure I fractured his jaw," McCaffey said. "He was coming into the punch and—well, it's no matter. The thing's done. Tell me something—and this is a blunt question to ask a man—but I heard that you've lived with the Apaches. Someone said something about a woman—"

"Somebody talks too much," Shotten said.

"Man, I'm not prying. I'm only trying to find some man who understands these Indians. To deal with them, we'll have to cross a language barrier first."

Mike Shotten shed some of his resentment. "All right, Linus. I didn't understand at first. I guess you know that Dan and I worked together for some time. We dealt with Cochise, sold him trade goods and Dan sold whiskey. I didn't know about that and when I found it out, it was too late."

"Too late for what? To back out? You did that all right."

"There was a girl," Shotten said. "She wasn't Apache, but Mexican, who had been taken as a small child. Of course she was Apache-raised, but her eyes were blue and her skin was fair and being in love was a natural thing, I guess. I'd have bought her and married her, but it never came to that. Dan peddled some whiskey to her people and the men got roaring drunk and one of them killed her. Cochise had him dragged to death behind wild horses for it, but it couldn't bring her back. That's when Dan and I went after each other with guns, but my aim wasn't the best and I only put him on his back for a couple of months."

"Dan Gannon's trouble always seems to be revolving around a woman," McCaffey said. "If my luck was that bad, I'd leave them alone."

"He can't help himself," Shotten explained. He got up. "Think I'll go down and muddy up the San Pedro while there's still some water in it. Did you know there's a spring not five hundred yards from here?"

"Yes, we found it," McCaffey said.

He got out his dispatch case and wrote a lengthy report, advising Captain Lovering that Shotten had arrived with men and materials and that construction would begin immediately. He also wrote a letter to Eloise, omitting the parts that would worry her; he sealed this, gave the packet to Noonan, and sent him on his way with instructions to ask for four more men and to come right back.

The cook had a big pot of beans, some hot biscuits, and coffee waiting when Shotten's men arrived. They were Mexican and the camp was filled with the babble of Spanish, a pleasant sound to McCaffey who had never heard it spoken before.

With workers, McCaffey could put his men off to stand guard duty, although all the Mexicans were armed, and in this way, get the adobe-making under way and the building walls up in a matter of weeks.

Shotten, on invitation, brought his cup and plate over to McCaffey, and sat down.

"How's the wound?"

"Coming along nicely," Shotten said. "I was really in a tight one the night I crawled into your barn. The damned bleeding wouldn't stop while I was moving. Then I fell off the horse." He shook his head. "My only regret was that I'd gone to Bessie's too early. Dan hadn't showed up yet."

"What's this—Bessie's?"

Shotten raised his eyes quickly. "You don't know? Why, I thought you—" He shrugged. "Bessie runs a whorehouse."

"Good Lord," McCaffey said, for he was a proper man who tried not to let life's roughness upset him. "My wife is bound to find that out. She's inquisitive, you know."

"I think she already knows," Shotten said frankly. "Linus, you've got a real woman there. Things don't throw her in a tizzy like they do most women. Did she tell you that she hit Al Gannon with a bucket and broke a paper bag of calcimine over Dan the first day she was in town?"

McCaffey stared. "My wife mercifully spares me some of these details. Three weeks before we were married she also horsewhipped a butcher in our home town because he kicked a little boy's dog."

Shotten laughed heartily. "And I'll bet she also told him you'd answer for anything she did."

"Exact— How did you know that?"

"I'm beginning to understand your wife," Shotten said. He finished his plate of beans, cleaned the plate with a biscuit, then drank some of his coffee. "The kind of woman a man needs out here are hard to come by. The kind he gets are like George Twilling's, prim around the mouth, hates dust, flies, Mexicans, coarse talk, and all men. The only reason they marry is because they hate the thought of being called an old maid."

"A man ought to leave that kind of a woman back East," McCaffey said. "Then when the country gets settled—"

"Nothing ever gets settled," Shotten said. "All my life I've been waiting for one thing or another to get settled. It never does. A man can stand by the side of the road and wait for the dust to settle, and about the time it does, a wagon will go by, or a man on a horse and he's got to wait all over again. You want kids, Linus, then have them. You take what comes and make the best of it and when it's all over, you'll find that it wasn't so bad after all." He finished his coffee and tossed the grounds away. Then he got up. "We'll start work after dawn. The Mexican foreman wants to know when the pay started."

McCaffey understood what Shotten meant, and said, "The hour the wagons started to roll."

Mike Shotten grinned. "You won't have any trouble with these men. That's what they wanted to hear."

7

DAN GANNON had not left his hotel room for a week, the time required to get the swelling to recede from his eyes so that he could peer through the puffed slits. And then only for a limited time for each morning they were puffed shut. Cold compresses usually opened them a little by mid-morning. Al Gannon was his nurse and he was getting tired of it, but wisely kept his brother from knowing this.

Al knew about his brother's vanity, and Dan would not show himself on the street until his face was completely healed. And he brooded about this for he knew that he had not marked Linus McCaffey, and he wanted to scar him badly, put a disfiguration on him to carry the rest of his life.

It also galled Dan Gannon to know that Shotten had escaped, and for a few days he had cursed his brother for his stupidity, but he finally admitted that it really wasn't his fault. Dan Gannon didn't want an open fight with the army.

Al was just finishing the job of shaving Dan, a delicate business considering the bruised tenderness of his face. "You really did right, Al," Dan said. "I want you to know that."

"After the way you cussed me out," Al said petulantly, "I wondered."

"I was just sore that Mike Shotten got away. Now I've thought it over. I'm not sore at you, Al. You did right." He snapped his fingers. "Put another damp cloth on my eyes."

"I just put a cloth—"

"I know what you did!" he shouted. "Now put another one over 'em!" He settled back and waited and Al did as he was told. "Oh, that feels good. This afternoon I want you to ride out and see Captain Lovering. You tell him how sorry you are that you made a fuss."

"I know what to tell him," Al said. "Stop acting like I was stupid. If it wasn't for me, you'd be dealing faro in New Orleans." He took the cloth away, wet it again, and slapped it not too gently across Dan's eyes.

"Hey! Take it easy!"

"You take it easy," Al said. "You've been playing the big shot so much you're beginning to think that you are. The trouble with you is that you get to doing something and forget what you're doing it for. Now I'll tell you flatly that we've put too much time into this, and too much money to lose it now. And Shotten's not going to step in and take what's mine either. It took us a year to stir up enough Indian trouble to where the army would be moved in. The army buys horses, food, supplies, and all this stuff has to be hauled and sold. There's the profit, stupid. The sutlers' license for all the posts in the territory is the gold mine. And the army is going to build eight posts. You figure that up, including the freight charges, and we're liable to make a million dollars."

"We ain't exactly got the license yet, have we?" Dan took the cloth off his eyes and peered at his brother. "You know, that Shotten, he ain't exactly dumb. He'd like to put his spoon in this dish too."

"You're going to get Shotten out of the way before the bids are opened," Al Gannon said. He turned to his hat. "I'm going out to see Captain Lovering because I'd already decided to go."

"There's no need to be mad at me, Al."

"No, I guess there isn't," Gannon said and went out.

He had his buggy hitched at the stable and drove out of town. It was a shame that Shotten had escaped, for they had laid their trap carefully. But McCaffey's wife had been an unexpected factor which threw them both off stride, and Al Gannon decided that the Lieutenant would have to be taken care of in some way to prevent him from butting in again. Of course, Dan and his stupid pursuit of women hadn't helped either, but there was no changing him; it was just something a man had to work around all the time and hope for the best.

At the post, the orderly took him to Captain Lovering's office. Al Gannon sat down and held his hat in his lap. Lovering's manner didn't seem overly friendly, and Al said, "I want to apologize for giving you trouble last week. Captain, I wouldn't have fired on the army. I honor that flag."

"Bullshit," Lovering said flatly. "What do you want, Al? The bids haven't been opened yet."

"Bids?" Gannon said. "Captain, I thought that Gannon and Gannon were the only ones who—"

"Shotten presented his bid," Lovering said. "Surprise you? It shouldn't. You've always feared he'd do that. Just another reason to put him out of the way." He turned around and looked at the wall calendar. "I've got three weeks, plus a day, in which to close the bidding." He turned back to Al Gannon. "You're going to have to wait. Shotten's willing to."

"He doesn't even have a license to operate as a sutler," Al Gannon said. "And I don't think the governor will give him one."

"We'll have to wait and see, won't we," Lovering said, smiling thinly. "Gannon, you look worried about this. Why should you be? Shotten's got a wanted dodger out on him, hasn't he? Or are you beginning to see how little weight that has, since your brother isn't really a sheriff, but just a handsome clotheshorse parading around for the women? Why don't you go to the governor? Dan's always bragged that he has a lot of pull."

"Gannon and Gannon can serve the posts better than any outfit in the territory," Al Gannon said. "What's Shotten got anyway? A ranch that's down at the heels, and Mexican help. You make a contract with him and you'll be sorry." He stood up. "I hate to be blunt about it, Captain, but it's the truth. Shotten's outfit simply can't do the job."

"The man may grow," Lovering said. "But we'll see

when we open the bids. Now if that's all, I have a lot of work to do."

Gannon went out, clapping his hat on his head, and he drove back to town in a sour frame of mind. Damn Mike Shotten and his gall, putting in a bid he knew he couldn't fill. The man didn't have the money to stock one store, let alone half a dozen.

He turned in his rig at the livery and went back to the hotel. Dan was standing before the mirror, lamenting the sad condition of his face. He turned away when Al came in and sailed his hat in a chair.

"That damned Shotten has put in his bid," Al said, lighting a cigar.

"He can't do that! He doesn't even have a license."

"No, and he's not going to get one," Al said. "I thought about it on the way in, and you're leaving for Prescott tonight. Shotten is bound to show up there to see the governor. Make damned sure that he doesn't."

"I don't want to travel in my condition," Dan said.

"Don't tell me that," Al said flatly. "Damn it, a gun is about all you're good with. You can leave as soon as it gets dark." He puffed furiously on his cigar, his brows wrinkled in thought. "You know, I thought it was damned funny that Shotten had the nerve to come back to Tucson after he'd been run out. And he had more of a reason than to visit Bessie's place. Hell, there's women across the border. To even apply for a sutler's license, he'd have to have someone vouch for him, someone reputable. By God, that's what he came in town for, to get someone to sign a letter."

"There's nobody in town that stupid," Dan said.

"The hell there isn't. The trouble with you is that you think you've got everybody scared. McCaffey's wife wasn't scared of you. Neither was her husband.

"He jumped me before I could get set."

"Did he really?" He laughed. "Leave tonight."

Lieutenant Linus McCaffey was very impressed with Mike Shotten and his crew of Mexican workers; they stayed on the job without constant supervision and the walls of the post went up ahead of schedule. Shotten kept an accurate check of the passing days as though he wanted to finish ahead of schedule, and McCaffey kept reminding him that there was plenty of time left, but Shotten didn't seem to believe that.

From their strange first meeting, a strong friendship was building between Mike Shotten and Linus McCaffey. Differing widely in background, they found they had much in common which had nothing to do with environment or culture. They were both strong men in a tough land, men who relied on themselves to solve their problems, and this similarity permitted them to talk of things they discussed with no one else.

McCaffey was not surprised when Shotten said that he had to leave for a week or so, although he didn't know the reason for it. They were sitting around McCaffey's supper fire, finishing their meal, and Shotten opened his pack sack and brought out a letter.

After reading it, McCaffey said, "I didn't know you'd put in a bid, Mike. And I surely didn't know that George Twilling had signed it."

"No one else does either," Shotten said. "If the Gannons knew, they'd kill George. I've got to see the governor and get a sutler's license in both our names. That's why I've got to leave now. Lovering's going to open the bids and if mine's to be any good, I'll have to have the license before he can accept it as final."

"I see," McCaffey said. "As a military man, I've been trained to expect the worst of the enemy. Thinking that way, I must assume that the Gannons know about the bid. In that case, you have to expect trouble in Prescott."

"That's my figuring," Shotten said. "I'll be looking for it too."

"Would you feel insulted if I sent Noonan and two other men along? Actually, I can cloak it under official business if you want to get technical."

Shotten laughed. "I'd like the company. But I thought maybe you'd like to go along."

McCaffey shook his head. "I couldn't leave this post. That's part of the army. Three men are the best I can do, and I'll be stretching a point out of shape to do that."

"I'll settle for that," Shotten said. "Better be on the watch for Indian trouble; likely Cochise has had his eye on you since the fight. He's got his pride and before he regains his honor among his people, he'll have to wipe you out."

"Yes, it makes sense, of a sort."

"Your detail's none too big as it is," Shotten pointed out. "With four of us gone, it may be enough to sway the balance of power in his direction. I say that to give you a chance to consider it and change your mind."

"I'm not much for changing my mind," McCaffey said. "When do you want to leave?"

"Night's best," Shotten said, "because the Apaches have some superstition about spirits wandering lost in the night. A man traveling has a better chance moving at night and staying holed up during the day."

"I'll tell Noonan to pick two more men and get ready then," McCaffey said. He fell silent for a moment. "Mike, does moving back into the Gannon territory mean so much to you?"

He shrugged. "I don't really give a damn about the Gannons, and it wouldn't bother me if I left them alone. But they won't have it that way. Maybe you don't understand their kind, Linus. They're out for all they can get and after they fill their pockets, they'll leave and let someone else clean up the mess. You can always tell their kind right off, because they never start anything. They let someone else start it, then they horn in on it. Tucson was there when they arrived, and they took it over. Someone found a little ore in the ground and they took that over. A Texan brought in the first herd of cattle and four months later the Gannons had it. Same way with the Indian trading. If they get their fingers in army business, they'll bleed the government dry before they can be stopped or run out."

"If I didn't know you better," McCaffey said, "I'd believe that you'd be content to leave them alone. But it's not so, Mike. You've got to kill Dan Gannon or he's got to kill you. I don't want to see it happen, but I don't know how to stop it."

"Don't try," Shotten said.

"Mike, I'll have to try. I don't give a damn whether Dan Gannon gets his lumps or not, but I don't want you to give them to him. You're going to get nothing out of it, Mike. Nothing at all, except maybe a rotten taste in your mouth. I've heard you're good with a pistol. Is that what you want to be remembered as? A man who was good with his pistol?"

"This is just talk," Shotten said. "You haven't lost anything to Dan Gannon."

"No, I haven't."

"Then you can't say what *you'd* do, or what I should do."

"True, but I can say what I'd like to think I'd do," McCaffey said. "Mike, I wouldn't want to be like you, and you wouldn't like to be the same as I am, but there's something in both of us that the other respects and admires. Let me put it this way. If I was going to do something that would hurt me, would you let me do it?"

"No," Shotten said. "Not unless it was something you had to do."

"Like killing Dan Gannon?"

"That's what I mean. It's just got to be done."

"Then let someone do it for that reason."

Shotten said, "That *is* my reason."

"No, your reason's dead."

He got up and stretched his legs. "Linus, I don't want to say any more about it. We're going to talk and get sore at each other and maybe fight about it and I don't want to do that. It's my business and I'll take care of it. Keep your nose out of it."

"If I'd kept my nose out of it I'd have let Al Gannon have you. You'd better think about that."

"I didn't think you'd ever remind me what I owed you," Shotten said.

"Mike, I wasn't."

"Sounded like it to me. Linus, I always pay off my debts."

McCaffey blew out a long breath. "You're right. We shouldn't talk anymore. I don't want to argue the point."

"No argument," Shotten said. "None at all."

8

Dan Gannon's intention was to leave town and not be seen by anyone, for his appearance hardly flattered him. Brother Al had the horse saddled and brought around to the rear of the hotel and tied up by the stairs, and after seeing that no one was around, told Dan to go on down. He had his blanket roll made up, and his rifle and sidearms; he mounted, said goodbye, and started out of town, taking the dark side streets.

It really was his intention to pass out unnoticed, but like many of his intentions, he lost them along the way. By coincidence he passed George Twilling's place and had just gone on when the door opened and Eloise Mc-Caffey stepped out, pausing in the full stream of lamplight.

Dan Gannon stopped and watched her say goodnight; she had evidently been invited to the Twillings for supper and was just about to go home.

Seeing her, Gannon couldn't keep his mind in line and the punishment he had already taken over her rose like a bitter wine and he knew that he had to get somethng for all his trouble. Eloise walked rapidly down the dark street toward her place and Gannon waited, then followed slowly so she wouldn't hear his horse walking in the dust.

The closer he got to her place, the wilder became his thoughts; she was a woman, young, shapely, pretty, and alone; the conquests he had known would be nothing compared to this. Whether he could get away with it or not never entered his mind, for he rarely thought of anything that far ahead.

She went in and when the lamp went on, he dismounted and tied his horse and walked carefully toward the adobe. There was one window at the front; he stopped there and looked in, but his view was almost completely blocked by the curtains she had hung.

Still he could see as she moved about the bedroom. He watched her slip out of her good dress and hang it and he had to take off his hat and wipe the sweat on his forehead. He put his hands against the glass as though he meant to part the curtains even though he couldn't reach them, and the window gave slightly. He almost laughed for he realized that this window was typical, a frame set into the opening and caulked in place with paper or rags; it wasn't really fastened to the building at all.

She was in the bedroom still, in her shift, combing her hair, and he gently eased the window in until he could get a grip on it. He had it out and was lowering it to the floor when it slipped and fell, shattering the glass.

Half in, half out, he decided to advance for the outer room was dark and he could grab her before she reached the door. Only she didn't break for the door. In a moment of horror he saw her snatch up a shotgun, point it in his general direction, and pull both triggers at once.

The recoil knocked her down; he got that much of an impression as a force slammed into him, mauling him, stunning him. He tried to claw his way out, but his right arm wouldn't respond and when he looked at it, he found it a limp, cloth-like appendage that dripped blood on the floor.

Then a blackness came over his mind and he dimly heard her opening the door and calling for help. Calling over and over again.

Three of Bessie's girls were the first to arrive. Bessie made her dress while one of the girls lighted a lamp. The yelling was attracting men now, a few of Bessie's customers, then several from town.

"Ain't that Dan Gannon?" Bessie asked. "Ruby, go get Doc Caswell. Hurry, girl. He's bleedin' like a stuck hog."

She rather took charge for she was a woman long used

to serious trouble. Eloise was crying, but she stopped when Bessie shook her roughly.

The men there were little use, except to get Gannon inside and stretched out on the table. Then Bessie ran them out and the doctor finally came.

With a scalpel he cut away Dan Gannon's coat, shirt, and undershirt, then frowned heavily. "God," he said, "what a mess."

Even though he knew Dan Gannon would never appreciate it, Caswell worked to save his life. The arm had to go, for there was little left of it to save, and Gannon was in shock now, so he didn't bother with ether. Bessie and one of her girls helped him with his work, and Al Gannon arrived but the men kept him outside for better than an hour and a half; it took Caswell that long to amputate, stop the bleeding, and probe for the stray buckshot in Dan's shoulder and chest.

A litter was made out of a door and four men carried him gently up town. Caswell went along, for he would have to attend him nearly every hour of the day and night now.

Bessie remained with Eloise but she shooed her girls back to her place, ever mindful that she was losing business and money.

Al Gannon came in, his expression dark. Bessie looked at him and said, "What the hell do you want?"

"I want to know what happened?"

"What does it look like?" Bessie snapped. "Go on, get out of here."

"There was no need to use a shotgun on him," Gannon said dully. He stared at Eloise McCaffey.

Bessie didn't like nonsense and she didn't like Al Gannon; she confronted him with her bulk and pointed to the broken window. "He pushed that out to get in. A man with honest business uses the door. Now let's see you make something out of that."

"If he dies," Al said, "I'll be back."

"You come back then," Bessie said. "I know how to reload a shotgun. And if I'd been shootin', he'd have lost his head instead of an arm." She gave Al Gannon a shove toward the door. "Get out before I throw you out." He retreated and she followed him and then she slammed the door and bolted it.

George Twilling came later; he'd just heard about it and got out of bed. He knocked and Bessie opened the door and Twilling showed his uneasiness in finding her there. He went to Eloise, saying, "Terrible. Simply terrible. But what could you do? A man's home is his castle. I hear Dan's in a bad way. May not pull through. Too bad. There'll be trouble over this. I know Al."

"Oh, why don't you shut up?" Bessie asked.

"I was only trying to help," Twilling said, his manner stiff, as though it somehow offended him to have to speak to her at all.

Bessie said, "Go on over and tell Ruby to give you a good time on the house."

Twilling's eyes got round and he glanced at Eloise McCaffey, his expression shocked. "My good woman, how dare you?"

Bessie laughed. "Ruby used to be your favorite."

He was a man caught and hating it; Twilling backed to the door. "Lies," he said. "You can't believe such lies." Then he hurried out and slammed the door.

"If anybody runs this town," Bessie said idly, "it ought to be me. I've got enough on most of the men to put them in hot water with their wives for the rest of their lives. Got anything to drink around here, honey?"

Eloise shook her head, and Bessie went to the window and whistled shrilly. Someone yelled, "Whatyawant, Bessie?"

"Bring a bottle of whiskey over here!" She turned back. "There's a time now and then when a drink is good for you whether you hate the stuff or not." She looked at Eloise's paleness, her drawn expression. "And you stop frettin' about what happened. There ain't a man in town who'd blame you for what you done. Dan asked for it once too often."

"I—I didn't really aim at him," Eloise said. "Then the gun knocked me down and he was just dangling there, half in, half out, blood running on the floor."

One of Bessie's customers brought the bottle, one of her private stock; she thanked him and got two glasses and poured. Eloise was instructed on how to drink it, fast, without a breath, and afterward, Bessie pounded her on the back while she tried to breathe and cry at the same time.

Then Bessie got her to bed and sat in a rocking chair the rest of the night, trying to remember back to a day when she'd been young and pretty enough to have a man go mad for her.

It was a long time and finally she gave up her foolish dreams.

She fixed coffee in the morning and made the younger woman eat. Eloise was no longer frightened; she had forced herself to take command again, and this pleased Bessie for she admired grit and hated cowards, whether men, women, or dogs.

Twilling and two other prominent men came; they wore suits and had shaved.

"Hate to disturb you," Twilling said, "but Al's demanded a hearin' and we've been selected—"

"All right, all right," Bessie said, half angry. "Where is it to be and when?"

"My store," Twilling said. "Within the hour."

"We'll be there," Bessie said.

Twilling seemed nervous. "No need for you to come, Bess—"

"I said, *we'd* be there. You want to say something else, George?"

"Said a sufficiency," Twilling admitted and went back to the center of town.

"Damn their hearin's anyway," Bessie said. "A lot of nonsense. Come on, honey. Let's not keep the good citizens waiting."

A good crowd filled Twilling's store by the time they got there, and a panel of five men had been selected to hear the facts of the matter. Al Gannon was there, and some women of the town who believed that where there was smoke there was fire, and they all looked Eloise

McCaffey over carefully and judged her by the company she kept.

Twilling acted as foreman and pounded for order. "We're here to look into the shooting of Dan Gannon. It ain't that he's been a model citizen, but—"

Al Gannon interrupted. "That's neither here nor there, George. Get on with it now."

Twilling scratched his beard. "I guess we'd better call Mrs. McCaffey to the chair. Will you step up here, please? Relate exactly what happened."

Eloise told them in a clear, strong voice. The first warning she had had was the shattering window and when she picked up the shotgun to fire, she had seen only the vague shape of a man and had not been able to identify him until after she called for help and someone —she couldn't remember who—had lighted the lamp.

Al Gannon had the right to ask questions and he sneered a bit as he looked at her. "Are you going to sit there and tell me that my brother tried to force his way into your house without some kind of an invitation from you?"

"I certainly am," Eloise said.

Gannon smiled. "Can you deny that you got kind of a swing when you walk that makes men look twice?"

"I'm not a man and I've never seen myself walk," Eloise said. "And can you deny that you've got a mind like a pigsty and a mouth all over your face?"

The men roared with laughter and Twilling had difficulty in getting them quiet. Al Gannon was angry now; he hadn't expected things to take this turn.

"Isn't it true that your husband and my brother fought over you?"

"It's true that my husband beat the daylights out of your brother," Eloise snapped. "Mr. Gannon, try what you want to twist this around to suit yourself, but I think now if I had known who forced my window, I'd have taken more careful aim."

"Just a minute here!" Bessie roared, surging her bulk erect. "Dan Gannon had his horse tied down the street, bedroll on and ready to go. Seems to me he was plannin' to leave town after he had his fun."

"He wasn't leaving for that reason at all," Al said quickly.

Twilling demanded order. "Sit down, Bessie; you're out of order."

"I ain't alone." She looked at Al Gannon. "Where was Dan goin' at night, sneakin' out of town?"

"He was not sneaking," Al said clearly. "Bessie, Dan was a vain man. He—ah—didn't want people to see him while his face was scabbed and cut up."

Twilling frowned. "Seems odd that he'd let Mrs. McCaffey see it." The others at the table nodded. "Al, it also seems that Dan's kind of been caught at his favorite game. Been long overdue, and that's the truth." He rapped the table. "I guess there's no more questions until Dan dies, if he does. Doc says he's got a fightin' chance but only a slim one. We'll close the matter now and if it has to be, we'll hold a trial later."

"Settle it now," Bessie said. "Twilling, you like to crawfish out of everything resemblin' trouble. Now make up your damned mind. This girl acted in self-defense or she didn't!"

Twilling shrunk a bit in his seat, then said, "I guess we agree that she done what any woman would have done." He rapped the table again and the meeting was over.

Al Gannon didn't think so. He came over to Eloise and said, "Girlie, you've got a man. But you won't have him long. I reckon I may as well start callin' you Widow McCaffey."

He frightened her and she showed it and this pleased him, but her fear was soon pushed back. She reached out and slapped him hard across the face. "I don't think you have the courage to face my husband down." She spoke loud enough for everyone in the room to hear, and they all listened carefully. "In my husband's name, I'm challenging you to meet him on the main street. I think you people have a name for it—calling a man out or something like that. You've wanted trouble since I first saw you. All right, Mr. Gannon, you can have what you want. Now you have my husband killed and every man in this town will know who ordered it." She smiled. "You're going to die like a man or a dog. I really don't care which way it is."

Then she pushed him aside and walked out of the store.

9

AL GANNON left Tucson late in the afternoon and headed for the mines, arriving just before dark. He put up his horse and went to the foreman's shack and had supper with him, beef and beans and half baked biscuits.

The mines were a Gannon enterprise, and although the silver was low-grade, the labor was cheap and there was really no capital investment for they had made no improvements since the days of Mangus Colorado nearly thirty years before.

The foreman was a man named Jakeson; he had never given a first name and neither of the Gannon brothers had asked for it. That Jakeson was on the dodge was no secret; most of the men working the mines were wanted by the law, and few for such gentle crimes as robbery or assault.

The mountains were a natural place for them, beyond the reach of the law; and Dan Gannon, in his trips to Chicago and San Francisco, dragged the gutters for the desperate, signing them for a year, binding them for twenty a month and board, and if a man broke away, he was always hunted down and brought back and punished by Jakeson.

No man ever ran away twice.

"I want twenty-five men for a job," Al Gannon said.

Jakeson stroked his beard. "Something extra in it?"

"Ten dollars a man."

"I can give you some mean ones for twenty-five," he said.

"I told you the price," Al Gannon said. "It's special

work. The ten men who do the job are free to leave without serving out their time."

Jakeson smiled. "You'll get ten easy. What's the job?"

"I want a raid carried off," Al Gannon said. "Get your map and I'll outline it for you."

Lieutenant McCaffey moved his command into the buildings and set up military housekeeping; he had already dispatched a rider to Captain Lovering, advising him that the post was ready for occupancy, and he was rather proud that it had been completed fifteen days ahead of schedule.

Mike Shotten had not returned, but McCaffey expected him at any time and had the guards alerted and watching for him. There was no sign at all of the Apaches, and this worried McCaffey, for the uncertainty of his position was more nerve-straining than an actual engagement.

Shotten and his men got back in the early evening; they were dusty and bearded and travel-worn, and Shotten came over to McCaffey's office to make a report.

He stepped inside and tossed his hat in a corner. "It beats all," he said. "There wasn't any trouble. None."

"Did you get your license?"

"Yes," he said and sat down. "I don't understand it. Dan and Al should have put up more of a fight." Then he laughed. "I'm not disappointed, Linus. Maybe we outsmarted 'em."

"I'd rather think it was something else," McCaffey said. "There's been no sign of an Apache for a week or ten days. That's worried me some for I've been cocked for an attack ever since you left." He fell silent for a moment. "They might be holding off to attack now, when the fort's finished."

"They don't think that far ahead," Shotten said. "When's the troops due to arrive?"

"Within a week, I'd say. Why?"

Shotten shrugged. "I ought to get back, but I'll hold my men here until the cavalry arrives." He grinned. "Or as long as the pay goes on."

One of the enlisted men came to the door. "Sir, there's

some activity out there that I don't understand. Sergeant Baker thinks it's Indians."

"Well let's have a look," McCaffey said, going out with his carbine in hand. One of the sentries had a pair of field glasses and McCaffey made his study before handing them back. "Indians, all right. Eight or ten and they're well-armed with rifles."

"That's odd," Shotten said.

Sergeant Baker came over, his manner unusually grave. "Somethin' odd here, sir. Apaches don't show themselves like that. And they're moving in, sir. I don't like it."

"Hell," Shotten said. "Who does?"

A rifle boomed two hundred yards out and one of the sentries clutched his chest and fell off his perch. McCaffey swore softly, and yelled, "Every man to his post! On the double now!"

The firing began, but McCaffey was forced to hold his, for the Indians were well concealed and good shots; two more men fell, one badly wounded, before he pulled his men into the best cover.

"Apaches don't shoot like that," Shotten said, and repeated it several times.

Whether they did or not was not McCaffey's worry; these Indians were shooting like crack infantrymen, and they were in a better position to attack than he was to defend.

We'll just have to take it, he thought, and get them when they try to breech the walls.

When darkness came, he expected a respite, remembering what Mike Shotten had said about the Indians not liking to fight at night, but he was again mistaken, for the Indians closed the distance and made an attempt to scale the walls.

The troopers managed to beat them off, and even killed one, but it did not stop the Indians for they kept up a sporadic fire all night, allowing no sleep except what could be taken in brief shifts.

McCaffey's welcome to the dawn was bleary-eyed for he had not slept at all. He had three dead men and one wounded now and he couldn't spare even one man. The

Mexicans were taking their turns on the palisade wall but none were eager to put their heads up and McCaffey couldn't blame them for they hadn't been hired to fight.

The light spread slowly, brightening, and he knew it was going to be a miserable day, and perhaps his final day. The cook managed to make coffee and serve breakfast, and the shooting seemed to taper off a bit, but McCaffey supposed this was his imagination, or wishful thinking.

Suddenly one of the Indians stood up and cried out and flung both arms behind him and as he fell, McCaffey could see the arrow protruding from his back.

It was a signal, for the air was suddenly thick with arrows, not directed at the post, but at the Indians hidden in the rocks. There was no sign, not even a glimpse of the men who shot the arrows, but the Indians were driven from their concealment, caught now between two hostile fires.

"Volley!" McCaffey shouted. "Fire in volley!"

It was a chance they had all been waiting for and the soldiers and Mexican laborers emptied their rifles. The Indians, driven into the open, had no chance at all, and in a minute the firing stopped for there was nothing else to shoot at.

Then, strangely, a handful of Apaches raised from their cover.

"Hold your fire!" McCaffey shouted, then tried to figure out why he had given that order; it had seemed instinctive, then he knew it was because none of the Apaches carried a rifle. They were all armed with bows and arrows.

The Apaches came toward the post and McCaffey signalled down for the main gate to be opened and he and Shotten went out to meet them. He recognized Cochise at a distance, and he came on alone while the others hung back.

Cochise spoke, and McCaffey understood none of it, and thought that it was a pity, for here was a chance to talk in peace with an Apache leader, and they could say nothing to each other. The Apache was intelligent and knew that McCaffey did not understand, so he motioned for him to follow and they all walked over to where one of the dead Indians lay.

Cochise rolled him over with his foot and then McCaffey said, "Why, they're white men!"

Shotten looked at several others, then came back. "I'm getting the slant of this now, Linus. This was supposed to look like Apache work, and Cochise was going to get the blame for it. It would have been the start of a nice Indian war after the Eastern papers got through printing the story of the massacre."

"Yes," McCaffey said. "Can it be that Cochise doesn't want to fight?" He offered his hand to the Apache who looked at it as though he didn't understand what it was for. Then McCaffey threw his carbine aside, and his pistol belt, and offered his hand again.

Cochise looked at it, then threw his bow and knife away and took the hand. A smile, McCaffey thought, might do it, and tried it, and in the Indian's eyes was an answering glint of pleasure.

Then he made a cup of his hand and raised it to his mouth and went through the motions of eating, and pointed to Cochise and then himself and the fort. The Apache got the idea of the invitation, and then the other Apaches came forward and they all went into the post together.

The Apaches were given food and coffee and McCaffey gave orders for the troopers not to flaunt their weapons around the Indians and make them nervous. Through hand motions, McCaffey was able to tell Cochise that he had a wife, and that he had no children. He learned that Cochise had a wife and two children. He managed to teach Cochise his name, and though the Apache pronounced it, "Mawcawpee," it was progress and McCaffey was pleased with it.

Cochise was persuaded to spend the night on the post and in the morning all the Apaches ate and then Cochise indicated that he wanted McCaffey to come with him. Shotten, who understood a little more of their ways than anyone else there, mentioned that the Apache would likely be insulted if McCaffey refused, so unarmed and alone, McCaffey went with Cochise to the Apache camp.

He was gone three days and Shotten worried, and before he returned, Captain Lovering arrived with two companies of cavalry. He was put out to find McCaffey missing and, by his manner, threatened unholy war when the young lieutenant returned.

McCaffey came back in the afternoon with Cochise, and in plain view of the fort and Captain Lovering, they shook hands and parted. McCaffey was whistling when he approached the gate and when he saw Captain Lovering standing there, he stopped.

"I am informed," Lovering said, "that that was Cochise. Is that true?"

"Yes, sir."

"You may resume whistling, Mr. McCaffey. Report to the office in a half-hour, after you shave. Good heavens, man, you smell like a wet wool blanket. Do Apaches smell like that?"

"Generally, sir."

"Bathe also," Lovering said and walked away.

He was working on a report when McCaffey came in and saluted. "At ease, Mr. McCaffey. My congratulations on a job well done. Shotten told me about the fake Indian trouble before he left."

"He's gone, sir?"

"Two days ago," Lovering said, smiling. "Mike Shotten's going to be a busy man, now that he's been awarded the army sutler's contract. Sit down, Linus. Tell me about Cochise."

"Well, I don't know much to tell, sir. You got my report on the initial trouble we had."

"Yes, and I expected to see you wiped out," Lovering said. "We've been out of touch, Linus. A lot has happened, here and in Tucson."

The way he said it made McCaffey suspicious, and a bit alarmed. "Concerning my wife, sir?"

"Yes," Lovering said and told him of the shooting. "Dan's going to live, but he'll be a one-arm man." He moved his own small stump. "To some it is a deep tragedy. Myself, I like to regard it as a turning point in my life. Frankly, my military career was run of the mill until I lost this. Then I fought to hold my rank, to stay in the service, and fighting, I distinguished myself. How this is going to affect Dan Gannon is anyone's guess. If it turns him sour, the territory is in for a real bad man."

"Is my wife all right?"

"Perfectly," Lovering said. "We wanted her to move onto the post but she wouldn't have it. A courageous woman, Linus. But I would move her here as soon as possible. In fact, I can relieve you of your duties for ten days so you can get that job done." He leaned back in the chair. "For the time being, you'll be assigned here. Not in command, naturally, and I'm sorry that I can't offer you something tactical, but setting up the sutlers on the other posts that will be built is a large job, a responsible job."

"Yes, sir," McCaffey said, barely hiding his disappointment.

"Of course, this is only temporary," Lovering said. "I have a great deal of faith in your administrative talents, Linus. Believe me, it's a lot easier for a commander to get a line charger than a good administrative man. I'm being advanced to major, you know. Expecting my orders any day now."

"Congratulations, sir."

"Thank you. I'm mentioning you in this report. It's about all I can do, Linus. With two years of service, you must be near the very bottom of the promotional list. But these things do count up."

"Yes, sir, and I appreciate it."

"You may start for Tucson any time you wish," Lovering said. "And I might warn you in advance that you'll likely find trouble. Your wife fairly ripped the hide off Al Gannon in public and told him that you'd meet him in the street any time he wanted it. He threatened to kill you. Called her Widow McCaffey. She's got a temper and a tongue, that woman." He smiled in a fatherly fashion. "I hope she doesn't get you in too deep, Linus."

"If the Gannons want a fight," McCaffey said, "I guess I can oblige them. Thank you for the warning. It's like Al to brace me the minute I hit town, and being in the dark, I might hesitate to use a pistol when he wouldn't falter at all."

"Do you have civilian clothes?"

"No, sir."

"A pity," Lovering said. "It looks bad, an army man fighting with civilians."

"They know who I am no matter what I've got on," McCaffey said.

Lovering waved his hand. "Yes, yes, I know, but it still looks better. Stop at my quarters and tell my wife to give you a suit of my woolens. And for heaven's sake, Linus, don't wear a holster with a flap on it."

10

AFTER THE BREAKFAST DISHES were washed and put away, Eloise McCaffey got out the washtub and began to get an early start on her laundry, and she was busy at this when she heard a horseman ride down the street and stop in front of her house. She started to dry her hands, then heard her husband calling for her and she ran to him and threw her arms around him. The dust on his clothes mingled with the water on her hands and when she touched his face she left muddy prints and they both laughed about that.

They went into the house and he stripped off his shirt and washed while she sat down at the table and watched him. "I've been lonesome for you, Linus," she said.

He looked at her and smiled. "Now and then I missed you too. Heard you had some excitement."

Her smile dimmed. "I said things I shouldn't have. Linus, I'm sorry."

"Don't be," he said firmly. Then he went over and pulled her to her feet and folded his arms around her. "If none of this had ever happened, I'd still have something to take up with Al Gannon." He told her about the raid. "The Gannons are always bragging about how they have control of everything. Then maybe they'll have an answer for me on this."

"There's some cold tea hanging in the well," she said. "Let me get you some."

"Just a glass before I go up town," he said.

She hesitated as though she had something to say, but she held it back and got the jug of tea and poured a glass for him. He drank and sighed and leaned back in

76

his chair. "Captain Lovering has given me permission to bring you back to Camp Grant," McCaffey said. "I'm to be stationed there, temporarily, of course." He drank the rest of his tea and put the glass aside. Then he got up and checked the loads in his Remington. "I don't think I'll be long."

She bit her lip and tightly clasped her hands together. "What would you like for lunch?"

He thrust the pistol into the waistband. "It's going to be too hot to cook. I'll get some cheese, or something." He bent and kissed her lightly, then went out.

She started to get up as though she meant to follow him, then she sagged back in the chair and put her face in her hands.

McCaffey walked to the central part of town and went directly to the saloon. Business was slack and the bartender came over as soon as McCaffey walked in.

"I'm looking for Al Gannon," McCaffey said. "Do you know where he is?"

"No," the bartender said. "Try the hotel."

"If you see him," McCaffey said, turning to the door, "tell him I'm looking for him."

"I'll do that," the bartender said. He watched McCaffey leave, then took off his apron and went out the back way. He hurried down an alley, then along a narrow side street to a small adobe. He knocked and a Mexican woman came to the door.

She said, "Al, he sleep now."

"You'd better wake him up. McCaffey's in town looking for him."

"You come inside," she said and closed the door after him. Gannon lay on a bed in one corner and she walked over to him and nudged him awake.

He sat up and looked at her, then at the bartender. "What's goin' on?"

"McCaffey's looking for you."

Al Gannon's face turned slack. "Get a horse and go to the mine. Tell—"

"You'd better take care of this yourself," the bartender said. "Al, you made the talk. You've got to back this one up alone or clear out. McCaffey's on the boil." He turned to the door, paused a moment, then went out without saying more.

Al Gannon washed his face and put on his shirt. Then he checked his pistol and buckled the belt around his waist. He shifted it first to the front, then to the back of his hip, then slid it around to a cross draw position, as though this was all strange to him.

"You no get yourself keeled," the woman said fearfully. "What happen to me then?"

"Bessie'll put you to work," Gannon snapped. "Leave me alone."

She began to cry. "You never marry me. Each week I must make confession." She tried to put her arms around him, but he brushed her aside and went out.

The sunlight was strong and he blinked, then he followed the alleys to the hotel. He entered by the back door and the clerk saw him and stopped him.

"That officer was in here—"

"I know all about it," Al Gannon said, his manner short. "Is the doc with my brother?"

"He hardly ever leaves," the clerk said. "If it wasn't for him, Dan would have been dead a—" He realized that Gannon was out of earshot, halfway up the stairs, and he went back to his counter.

Doctor Caswell answered the door, but he blocked it so that Al Gannon could not get in. "What do you think you want, Al?"

"I want to talk to Dan."

Caswell shook his head. "He's so full of morphine to kill the pain that he couldn't talk to anyone." He smiled thinly. "I saw McCaffey moving around town. What did you want Dan to do, get him with a rifle from an upstairs window?"

"Smart mouth, ain't you?" He turned and went down the hall and Caswell closed the door.

McCaffey came from George Twilling's back room where he had changed from his uniform to civilian clothes. He looked at the wrinkles and felt uncomfortable in their stiffness. Twilling said, "The sizin' washes right out, Lieutenant. I'll wrap your other things for you."

"I'll pick them up later," McCaffey said. He went to the door and stood just inside, so he could see most of the street. "The town isn't very big, but I'd hate to have to hunt through every adobe to find him."

"Seems to me it'd be more sensible to wait and have him come to you," Twilling said.

McCaffey turned his head and looked at him. "George, this town doesn't need either one of the Gannons. I'll take the trouble to him, and either way, he's going to be finished in Tucson. I don't want to sound like some political office-seeker, but as long as you have Al and Dan Gannon running things here, you're going to have a cluster of adobes separated by dusty streets and little more."

"I know that," Twilling said. "But what can a man do? You give the Gannons trouble and the miners come in and wreck your place. It's happened. That's how he pulls people in line."

"He can't do that to the army," McCaffey said.

He saw someone step out of the hotel and his attention sharpened, then he moved out of Twilling's place and paused in front. Thirty yards away, Al Gannon took advantage of the shade, and he didn't see McCaffey until he spoke.

"Over here, Al." He stepped to the street and started to cross over, and Al Gannon simply stared for a moment, then jerked his pistol free of the holster. He fired once, wildly, and missed and wheeled back into the hotel before McCaffey could get his own pistol out of his belt.

McCaffey broke into a run and made the walk and paused there to think this over. Gannon had the advantage of being inside the building and was probably waiting to shoot anyone who tried to come through the door. Yet McCaffey knew that he couldn't just wait and let this thing come to a stand off. The essence of military maneuvering was to press any attack launched and never give the enemy a chance to entrench, or to think it over.

He found a stick near the walk and picked it up, then swung it wide and flung it through the front window. Immediately a pistol shot followed the falling glass and while Gannon's attention was thus focused, McCaffey boiled through the doorway. He landed in a tumbling roll that carried him behind the clerk's counter, and Al Gannon fired again, but he was late.

The clerk, no longer feeling safe, threw his arms over his head and rushed out, yelling for Gannon not to shoot him. A crowd was forming on the street, but no one came in.

McCaffey said, "Do you want to stand up, Al? You might be lucky and get me."

"I'll get you," Gannon said.

McCaffey tried to position him from the sound of his voice, and couldn't, so he risked a quick look and saw Gannon crouched behind an overturned sofa. Gannon snapped another shot and chipped wood off the clerk's desk, and ducked down, thinking that McCaffey would do the same.

Only he jumped free of the desk and caught Al Gannon flat-footed. Gannon started to cock his pistol, but McCaffey said, "Don't be that foolish! I'll have a bullet in you before you can get your thumb off the hammer."

Gannon started to put his gun down, but McCaffey shook his head. Gannon said, "What do you want then?"

"Keep your pistol. Walk ahead of me to the street. Try any time you want to."

"I'm not that stupid." He got to his feet and went out and stopped for everyone in Tucson was facing the front of the hotel.

"Walk to the center of the street," McCaffey said. He held his gun at arm's length and when Gannon had gone far enough, he said, "Stop there. Keep your back to me." He let Gannon stand there for a moment. "Al, I counted your shots. At best you've got two left. I haven't fired at all, but that doesn't matter. Keep your gun hanging by your side. Now cock the piece. Mine is cocked and held the same way. You can turn and face me and fire any time you want."

"With a gun at my back?"

Twilling spoke up. "He ain't lyin'. Better take it, 'cause you'll never get a fairer chance."

"There's nothin' to keep him from shootin' me five times," Al Gannon said. "He's got full chambers. I've got one shot left."

"That can be fixed," McCaffey said and discharged his pistol in the air four times. Then he dropped it alongside his leg. "You'd better turn around now or start crawling."

"I don't crawl to any man," Gannon snapped. He wheeled fast and shot and the bullet missed McCaffey by inches. Then a look of horror came over Al Gannon's face and he inclined his body as if to bolt, but froze when McCaffey spoke.

"You'd never live to take the second step!"

"God, you just can't execute a man," Gannon said softly.

"Why not? Didn't you tell my wife you were going to make her a widow?"

"I was mad then!"

"I'm mad now," McCaffey said calmly.

Some of the men laughed and Gannon shook his head. "Give me another gun, somebody."

"How many chances do you want?" McCaffey asked. "You had one when I crossed the street, and three in the hotel, and another on the street just now. I think you're long on mouth and short on guts. Am I right, Al?"

"You're right," Gannon said.

"Tell them then."

He shook his head, then thought better of it. "I'm short on guts."

"A man like you shouldn't have anything to say about this town," McCaffey said. "I'll leave it up to these men if they want to buy you out. You're through here, Al. Finished. I'll give you your life and whatever these men want to offer you for what you own. Better take it."

"If Dan was—"

"He isn't," McCaffey snapped. "And when he gets on

his feet, I'll tell him the same thing. I'm going to be in town three days. When I leave, you'd better have already gone." He looked at the men lining the street. "How many of you have had enough of the Gannons?"

There was murmur along the street; they were getting some courage now. George Twilling came up to Gannon and shook his fist in his face. "I'm partners with Mike Shotten. How do you like that?"

"So that's who he got," Gannon said. He started to turn, but Twilling grabbed him by the collar and hit him in the face. It was a signal and they crowded him and mauled him until their old angers were satisfied. McCaffey pulled clear of this and Twilling came up; he had some of Al Gannon's blood on his knuckles and he seemed happy about it.

"Never thought I'd see the day when their hold was broken," he said. Then he looked at McCaffey and smiled. "I never knew it would break so easy."

"Who said it was easy?"

Twilling frowned. "Didn't look hard to me."

"Then the next time, you carry your own gun," McCaffey said.

He walked home and went into the adobe. Eloise wore an anxious expression, and when she saw that he wasn't hurt she let down with relief and began to cry.

"Now you don't want to do that," he said gently.

"I heard the shooting."

"He was a bad shot," he said. Then he put his arm around her. "He'll leave town."

It was a relief to her that he hadn't killed Gannon. "Then it's all over."

"Postponed," he said. "Dan Gannon will get well. They'll set up somewhere else. I only put off until to-morrow what I should have done today. But then, it was my first time home in a while and I didn't want anything on my mind but you."

"Oh, you're terrible—I'm happy to say."

11

MIKE SHOTTEN arrived in Tucson late in the afternoon and stopped at the saloon for a glass of beer and he had hardly finished it before he heard the whole story of McCaffey's stand-off with Al Gannon. Shotten left the place, and rode over to McCaffey's adobe; he found the lieutenant loading a wagon.

Shotten grinned and said, "I thought it was Gannon who was leavin' the country."

"We're moving to Grant," McCaffey said. "Step down, Mike." He turned his head and called to his wife who was inside. "Eloise, Mike's here!"

She came out as Shotten swung down. "It's nice to see you," she said. "How's your wound?"

"Oh, completely healed, or nearly so," he said, brushing dust from his clothes. "I've got eight wagons to load at Twilling's store, so if you can delay until tomorrow, I'll go to Grant with you."

"We can use the company," McCaffey said. "Come in. This sun's hot and Eloise has some tea in the well." They went in and Shotten removed his brace of pistols and put them aside, a custom of the country when friends got together. When Eloise poured the tea, McCaffey said, "As soon as I get to Grant, I'm going to take measures to have a properly constituted legal authority established in Tucson. This little stigma that Dan Gannon's put on your name has to be removed."

Shotten laughed. "You mean, my being wanted by the law?" He shook his head. "I wouldn't pay any attention to that, Linus. It's only Dan who—"

"Yes, but he had fliers printed up and sent around.

83

You're a contract sutler now, Mike. The matter will have to be taken care of."

"All right," Shotten said. "You figure out how."

"I will," McCaffey said.

He let the subject drop and they talked of other things, of the troops already moving to Grant, and the supplies being hauled in. A quartermaster wagon train was leaving that evening, loaded to the top boards with uniforms and saddles and all the things armies carry around with them.

Shotten had new and important responsibilities and he was a man who took them seriously. As sutler, he was the beef contractor for the post and supplied the mess as well as the sutlers' store. When other posts were built, his job would increase fivefold, but he was planning for it, expanding his operation as rapidly as possible. There was a risk involved, for if he failed to keep his contract, the army would cancel it and he and Twilling would be left with a heavy debt and a large inventory, enough to break both of them.

After supper, and before it got dark, they finished loading the wagon, and Shotten stayed the night, sleeping again in the small barn. And in the morning, Eloise fixed breakfast and they moved out of Tucson before the town came awake.

There was, McCaffey decided, no poorer way in the world to travel than by wagon, for the trail was terrible and the jolting was almost beyond endurance. He was fortunate in being mounted, and after two hours he took Eloise off the wagon and made her ride double with him.

They camped the night along a small creek, not far from the trail; cook fires were built up and Shotten put out guards before coming over for his supper. He sat down and filled his plate, then said, "Habit's hard to break, Linus. A man keeps looking for Apaches even when he knows they're not raiding." He looked at Eloise and grinned. "I didn't hear a complaint from you at all today. Women and wagons are usually—"

"What good would complaining do?" she said. "This is only temporary."

"A favorite saying of ours," McCaffey said. He put his arm around her. "When we're in the middle of something we don't particularly like, we always say that it's only temporary. Somehow it never seems so bad."

"We used to do that when father's pay didn't quite stretch far enough," Eloise said. "The situation was only temporary."

"I'll have to try that," Shotten said.

There was a commotion at the fringe of the camp and they turned and looked that way but darkness was too thick for them to see. Then one of Shotten's men came up in a hurry. "Trouble," he said and McCaffey and Shotten went with him.

A man lay on the ground, bleeding from a bad wound and he wore no clothes except his underwear. One of Shotten's men brought a lantern and shined it down, and another gave the man water. He looked around for a moment, then saw McCaffey and recognized him and tried to draw himself to attention.

"Private—Shannon—sir." He tried to salute and fell back; McCaffey took off his neckerchief and wet it and washed the man's face.

"What happened, Shannon? Take your time, man. Give him some more water there. And a drink of whiskey if there's any in the camp."

He had been shot through the side and calf of the leg and these wounds were washed and bandaged; all the while he talked in halting phrases.

"It was dusk—sir. No chance—at all. Twenty men or—more—jumped us. All dead—sir. Twelve men—all dead."

"What did you have in the wagons?" McCaffey asked.

Shannon shook his head. "Damned funny there—sir. Nothin' of value—to anyone but—army. Mess supplies and —uniforms and—quartermaster gear." He sagged back in a man's arms and a drink of whiskey was poured down him.

Mike Shotten said, "Carry him over to a wagon and rig a hammock for him." He walked back to the fire with

McCaffey. Eloise wore a concerned, puzzled expression.

McCaffey said, "The quartermaster wagons were hit by bandits and looted. There was one survivor."

"Yes, and he was an oversight," Shotten said grimly. "Linus, what the devil was the point? Did they mistake it for something of more value?"

"I don't know," McCaffey said. "Mike, can you spare a man to ride with a report to Captain Lovering?"

"Sure," Shotten said, and poured a cup of coffee, but held it in his hand and stared at the fire.

Al Gannon and his men returned to the mines late at night and they worked for an hour unloading the pack horses and carrying the boxes and bundles into the supply shed. Then they broke them open and Gannon said, "Every man is to outfit himself completely. Be ready to ride in an hour."

"Ain't we had enough for one night?" one man asked.

Gannon looked at him. "You want to pay the Apaches back, don't you? All right then, shut up. I'm going into town. I'll be back in time to ride with you."

He went out and mounted his horse and went into town. He tied up in back of the hotel and went up the stairs without attracting any attention to himself, then he let himself into Dan Gannon's room.

Doctor Caswell was asleep in a chair and Al Gannon woke him by kicking his foot. Caswell snorted and came awake and Gannon said, "Out. Go on, get out. I want to talk to my brother."

"He's sleeping."

"Then I'll wake him," Al Gannon said. "Go get a cup of coffee or something."

Caswell hesitated, then got up and went out and Al Gannon turned up the lamp. Dan Gannon's appearance was a shock for the man had lost twenty pounds and his color was bad and he looked five years older. He opened his eyes and looked at Al Gannon, then smiled.

"How you feelin' there, boy?" Al asked.

"Meaner by the day," Dan said." Another two weeks

and I'll be able to get out of this bed. Then I'm going to kill a woman."

"I ain't been sittin' on my hands since you got hurt," Al said. "Tonight we raided an army wagon train and stole a whole bunch of uniforms and gear."

"What for?"

"So we can raid the Apache camp and make them think the army's betrayed 'em." He pulled a chair close to the bed and sat down. "Cochise will be foamin' at the mouth and he'll raid everything in sight. And while he's doing that, we'll start hitting Shotten's wagons and let the Apaches take the blame for it. When he's out of business, we'll be back in business. The more trouble the Apaches cause, the more army will be sent here to put it down, and the more soldiers, the more supplies they'll need. We'll be rich as hell, Dan."

"You save that woman for me," Dan said. "I want your promise, Al. I'm going to kill her myself."

"Let the Apaches do it."

Dan Gannon shook his head. "No, I want to do it." He stirred the stump of his arm. "She made me half a man. I'd rather be dead than half a man."

"You just get well," Al said, rising. "I've got to go. We're going to raid Cochise before dawn."

"You take care of yourself, you hear?"

"Sure," Al said and went out. He found Doctor Caswell in the lobby. "You can go up now."

"Why, thanks," Caswell said sarcastically.

Al Gannon frowned, then said, "Any price you want, doc, you just name it."

"I didn't do it for money," Caswell said. "But I'm not going to explain that to you."

"All right, suit yourself. Just so he gets well, that's all I care."

"Al, he's not ever going to be really well," Caswell said. "From here on in, he's going to have to have medicine regularly. Day and night he had to be kept under the influence of morphine. That has a lasting effect on any man."

"So he's got to take pills," Al said. "Look, I'm in a

hurry. You just fix him up with what he has to have. All right?" He thumped Caswell on the chest and hurried out the back way.

He rode back to the mine and found his men waiting, dressed in army uniforms. Gannon laughed and put one on himself, then fumbled with the saber as he mounted.

"I don't see how a man can ride with all this junk," he said and turned out, leading his men toward the mountains.

They rode out the rest of the night, stopping only long enough to rest the horses. An hour before dawn, Gannon dismounted his gang and they went the rest of the way afoot, working slowly along the ridge flanking a small valley and spring. The Apache hogans were below them, and in the faintly increasing dawn light they could make them out.

Gannon gathered them near and said, "Now we don't have to kill them all. Spread out and wait until the camp starts to stir. I'll fire the first shot well after daylight. Everyone stand up to fire so they can see the uniforms. Do it in a line, like the army does. We'll let loose one good volley then get the hell out of here. Everybody understand that?"

They did, but one man had a question. "Wouldn't it be all right to kill a squaw or two?"

"Go ahead if you feel like it," Gannon said. "All right, spread out, but not too far apart."

He bellied down to wait, cradling his rifle in the crook of his arm. It was good to be killing something. He thought of Linus McCaffey and it was a hard acid in his stomach, the hate that he felt for this man, for McCaffey had taken all his weaknesses and held them up and made him look at them, acknowledge them when he wanted badly to deny that he had any at all.

It was good to think of the outcome of all this, and he could see it vividly, the flare of Cochise's anger at having been betrayed, and his reprisals against the army. The story was going around that Cochise had taken McCaffey to his camp, and soon Cochise would regret this for he would believe that McCaffey had used that knowledge to pull this raid. All the inert suspicions and hate for the white man would come to the fore, and McCaffey, not suspecting a thing, would be a sitting duck when the Apaches attacked.

To Al's thinking, it was a beautiful plan, almost in the realm of genius, and he'd have to remind Dan of this from time to time because Dan was prone to forget these things. He could get pretty irritated with Dan because Dan always thought of himself first and someone else later.

That'll have to change, Al thought, and watched the camp.

The dawn was quite bright and there was a stirring below, but still he waited. Some men left their hogans and a dog barked, then the women began to appear, gathering wood and building up the fires.

He figured that this was the time, so he stood up, shouldered his rifle, and dropped a young brave with one shot. Instantly the camp boiled with activity, women yelling, men yelling and racing for their weapons, and along the ridge, a dozen men in army blue formed a line and fired a wicked volley into the Apaches.

A woman fell, and three men, and a small boy who had been running for the safety of his hogan. Al Gannon couldn't accurately count the dead, and he didn't want to; his only thought now was to get out and get out fast for he felt a fear grip him, a horror of being trapped in the mountains, captured by the Apaches, for he had no wish to die with his face tied to a bag of hot ashes.

He led the retreat to the horses and they mounted hurriedly, turned and rode fast. Then he had hardly gone more than a mile when he realized that he had make a mistake. The long night march had tired the horses, worn their stamina thin, and they began to breathe hard, unable to set the kind of pace he wanted.

They'll catch me, he thought and it made fear a pain in his head. Yet there was no choice; he dismounted, as did the others, and they led the horses, keeping in the rocks where they would leave no sign, and hoping that the Apaches wouldn't catch up with them.

12

Sergeant Baker came from the post with a detail to meet Mike Shotten's wagons, and he seemed pleased to see Linus McCaffey; they rode on into the post and Baker saw that Eloise was taken to suitable quarters while Linus McCaffey reported to the officer in command.

Lieutenant Burchard was in command, and eager to get rid of it; he offered McCaffey a cigar, then said, "I've awaited your arrival with some anxiety, Mr. McCaffey, for I have orders to return to Tucson and turn this command over to you."

McCaffey could not conceal his surprise. "But I thought—"

"Yes, well, Lovering's changed his mind. You'll find everything in order. You have D Company, Lieutenant Powers in command. A Company, commanded by Lieutenant Heffernan. Quartermaster supply—well, here's a list. You can meet them later. Good luck."

"Excuse me, but you seem in a hurry."

"Hell yes. My request for leave has been approved. My wife and I will be starting East in two days."

"I hope you have a good trip," McCaffey said. "And I can't say that I'm sorry to see you go for I've wanted a tactical command for two years."

"You're welcome to this one," Burchard said. "I'll be cleared out in an hour."

"There's no hurry."

"Your point of view," he said.

McCaffey assumed his command informally and he found that he was not nervous about it, as though he had been doing this off and on for life. He met the other officers on the post, and the important sergeants, and his only moment of uneasiness was knowing that he was junior officer to three lieutenants. But that often happened in the army, and he shrugged it off.

He was proud of his post, proud of the solid construction and the accommodations, yet he expected the enlisted men to bitch about it for the location was a bit desolate and the summer heat was a constant oppression.

Burchard cleared the post promptly, and McCaffey secured it and went to his new quarters. Eloise was unpacking and she straightened and rubbed a small kink in her back.

"I don't know whether I'm going to wear the trunks out first, or the contents. There must be more to life than packing and unpacking."

"I thought Noonan was helping you."

"He went to get a box of groceries," she said, and sat down. "He told me you were the commanding officer."

"Yes. Burchard left." Linus McCaffey smiled. "Frankly, I feel damned good about it. Ambitions realized, and all that nonsense."

"You're going to do very well," she said. "Now help me with this mess."

Noonan returned and she made some coffee and cheese sandwiches and the three of them worked until mid-afternoon, then Sergeant Baker came to the quarters and knocked.

"Sir, there's some Apaches approaching. Cochise, I think, and they're carrying the dead."

"Dead?" McCaffey ran out and mounted the wall. The Apaches were still several hundred yards away and he called down to the sentry. "Open the gates. Fetch my horse."

"He's not saddled, sir," Baker said.

"Damn it, get me any horse then."

One was brought up and he rode out and a moment later Baker followed. The Apaches stopped and drew back their bows as McCaffey flung off. He looked at the dead, the woman and the two children, then he looked at the hate in Cochise's eyes. Twenty arrows and a few muskets pointed at his heart, yet he felt no fear at all, just a sorrow that this had happened and he reached out to touch the woman Cochise held in his arm. Instantly a brave thrust a knife point to his throat and stopped him.

Again the language barrier stood like a wall between them. Cochise spoke his name, "Mawcawpee," and spat. Baker said, "He blames you for this, sir."

"Ridiculous, but obviously you're right."

The woman was taken from Cochise's arms, and he gestured, talking rapidly, angrily. He finally took McCaffey's sleeve and pointed to the cloth and then made shooting motions.

McCaffey said, "My God, he says that soldiers did this. Sergeant, have there been any patrols away from the post?"

"None, sir. Positively none."

It was not easy to convey to Cochise what he meant, but McCaffey pointed to himself and Baker and the post and held up his fingers to indicate the soldiers there, and made shooting motions and all the time shook his head, and in this way denied a part in this murder.

Cochise did not believe it, and he gestured and they could make out his meaning: he meant to attack the post and kill them all.

Again and again McCaffey protested his innocence, but it had no effect upon Cochise; his mind was made up and he no longer believed McCaffey.

"Sergeant, get me the rope off the saddle," McCaffey said. He took off his pistol belt and threw it on the ground, then his shirt and undershirt and hat. Baker stood there with the rope and McCaffey said, "Tie my hands behind me, sergeant, then hand the rope to Cochise. But make the motions I've made, that I did not do this, and neither did the soldiers. Show him, if you can, that if he must kill, he kills an innocent man."

"I wouldn't do that, sir. Understanding ain't too good as it is and he's liable to—"

"Do as you're told, sergeant!" He put his hands behind him and Baker tied the knots; McCaffey talked while he worked. "Tell my wife not to worry, that I'll work this out some way. Whoever did this killing has to be caught and punished. Tell Lieutenant Heffernan that he's in command until I return."

"He may roast you over a slow fire before you—"

"I know the risks," McCaffey said, "and they are less by far than having him attack the post."

He took the end of the rope from Baker and handed it to Cochise who yanked savagely, spun McCaffey around and threw him to the ground. The Apaches let out a joyous whoop, and Baker said, "I ain't gonna let 'em take you, sir."

"I gave you an order, damn it," McCaffey said, getting to his feet. "Return to the post, sergeant. Damn it, move!" He pointed to himself, then to Cochise, and made a motion that they would go together, and that was exactly what Cochise had in mind. One of the Apaches scooped up McCaffey's pistol belt for weapons were hard to come by, and they turned away.

An hour carried them deep into the hills, and there they stopped and the dead were taken away and McCaffey waited, guarded by Cochise and four Apaches.

Finally they moved again, walking fast, and McCaffey was hard pressed to keep up. By nightfall they reached a temporary camp high in the mountains, and when the women and children saw the prisoner, they fell on him with switches and sticks and beat him unconscious.

When he woke, he found himself bound hand and foot and sleeping on a manure pile. He must have made some sound, for Cochise came in the hogan, stirred him with his foot, then cut his legs free so he could stand and follow him outside.

He brought forward a small boy of eight or ten, who looked at McCaffey with dark, fearless eyes. Every man in the camp was gathered around the fire, waiting, then Cochise spoke to the boy.

And the boy surprised McCaffey by speaking in poor, but understandable English. "I am Yazzi, not of these people. I am Yuma. Many years I live with white woman. Speak good talk, no?"

"The sound of your voice," McCaffey said, "is purely beautiful, Yazzi. You speak Apache?"

"Yes. Cochise asks whether it would insult you to have a child speak your words."

"You can speak for me," McCaffey said.

The boy related this to Cochise, who had a great deal to say. Yazzi translated it. "Cochise promises you a slow death. Your feet will be bound in hot ashes. Then your hands. Then your face. One of the dead women was his sister."

"The soldiers did not kill her," McCaffey said.

This was repeated and answered and repeated again. Yazzi said, "Many eyes saw the soldiers in blue on the ridge. They stood for all to see."

Again McCaffey denied this, but Cochise was not ready to believe him. Then he began to gain an insight into these people, and he felt that he could bargain, but he would have to offer them a prize worth waiting for, something enticing, that would appeal to their savage appetite for torture.

"Yazzi, tell Cochise that he has nothing to gain by killing me now. Tell him we will hunt together the men who pretended to be soldiers. Ask him if this is not possible. Ask him if he remembers the white men who pretended they were Apaches. Why could not men pretend to be soldiers?"

This was relayed, and it made some impression on Cochise; he wanted to know what McCaffey had in mind and only then did the notion of dying slowly leave McCaffey.

"Tell Cochise that if we hunt together and my words prove false, I will give him my eyes to be taken one each day, and a finger a day, and a toe a day, and my tongue on the last day."

Yazzi repeated this and Cochise thought it over, then agreed, and Yazzi translated his words. "He says that he will hunt from moon to moon. I am to be taken along to speak the words." He bulged his little chest with pride. "I may even become a man because of this deed and be given a new name."

"You're a good man now," McCaffey said.

His wrists were freed, still he was guarded while Cochise left to get his water bag and rifle. He came back, wearing McCaffey's pistol belt and Yazzi was given a knife to wear, a thing that made him dance for joy.

Cochise put his hand on the boy's shoulder and spoke to him at length, and when he was through, McCaffey said, "What did he say?"

"He told me that I must run like a man and never to tire or show pain. I must be brave at all times for Cochise will be watching me, and you will be watching me, and that I must die like an Apache."

"Those are hard words of advice for a boy," McCaffey said.

As a soldier, he would have rested before starting out on a journey of uncertain duration, but it was not the Apache way; they were like animals, resting when there was time, and storing strength for times of battle.

McCaffey was without weapons, and he walked behind Cochise, with the boy following, running most of the time to keep up. There were no rest periods and even in the darkness, Cochise knew every trail, and moved with uncanny accuracy. Toward dawn they stopped on a high ridge and Cochise spoke, Yazzi translating.

"It is the spot where the soldiers stood and fired," the boy said. "We will stay here until daylight."

McCaffey slept Apache style, on the ground, without a cover, shivering in the dawn chill, and he did sleep, even when he thought it impossible. A gray light woke him and he sat up. Cochise was standing nearby and he offered his water bag.

As the light grew better, they examined the ground and found the prints of government issue boots clearly indented into patches of soft earth. It was proof to Cochise that the soldiers had killed his people, but McCaffey noticed one thing, and pointed it out to Cochise.

"Each boot mark is new, Cochise. The threads and nails in the soles are plain to see. Every soldier does not get new boots at the same time just as every Apache does not get a new knife or new moccasins. A train of army wagons carrying uniforms was attacked and all but one were killed. Those who attacked the wagons could be wearing the soldier uniforms."

Yazzi conveyed this to Cochise, who saw some merit in the argument, yet was not convinced.

They went on, carefully following the faint sign until they found where the horses were kept hidden during the attack, and McCaffey then felt that he had something Cochise might believe.

"The tracks are not the same," McCaffey said. "Army horses are shod with a regulation shoe. Cochise has seen the print many times, and they are all the same. These horses were shod by several men and with different kinds of shoes. Has Cochise ever seen the army ride horses that were not so many hands high, as alike as can be found?"

To a man who spent his life correctly reading the small signs in the trail, this was a potent argument. Cochise turned to McCaffey and took the pistol from the holster and cocked it. He held the muzzle inches from McCaffey's face and spoke through Yazzi.

"I will ask the question and you will answer and I will see the truth or lie in your eyes. If I see the lie, I will kill you instantly."

"Tell him to ask his question," McCaffey said.

Yazzi repeated it, then stood there with his eyes round and staring.

Cochise spoke, and the boy said, "Did any soldier from the post kill the Apache women?"

"No," McCaffey said, shaking his head. He looked directly at Cochise when he spoke, and he staked his life on this man knowing the truth when he heard it.

For a span of ten seconds Cochise held the pistol steady, then he lowered it off full cock, holstered it, and handed the belt to McCaffey. Then he put his hand on Linus McCaffey's shoulder and said, "We will hunt the men together, the Apache way. Have you the stomach for this?"

"Tell him," McCaffey said, "that it will be done the way of Cochise. Tell him he does not lead me and I do not lead him. Tell him we walk side by side, the three of us." He put his arm around the boy's shoulder and stood that way while his words were translated.

It brought a smile to the Apache's face, a brief fleeting sign of approval, then he moved on, again the most relentless, the most savage of all animals.

13

LINUS McCAFFEY's education began the moment he started this journey with Cochise, and it was something he had never dreamed of learning, how the Apaches could live off the land in this wild country. When Cochise became hungry, he searched the mesquite thickets for small mounds of earth piled by burrowing rats. Yazzi explained that the rat had many enemies and his burrow was always a maze of holes to trap snakes, and yet supply an escape route other than the one occupied by the intruder. Cochise, being well informed on the rat's habits, blocked off all the holes but one and had McCaffey and Yazzi poke sticks down the burrow until the rat came out. A swung stick killed the rat, then he was gutted and thrown on a bed of coals, which burned off the hair and cooked the meat.

The Apaches knew where the mescal pits were, for baking it was a two- or three-day job and what remained was left for someone else. Cochise knew of one close by and McCaffey couldn't decide whether he liked the taste or not. He decided that it had the flavor of molasses candy, but it was tough and grainy.

He learned to eat nopal and the fruit of the Spanish bayonet and the seeds of sunflowers, and in the high swales, a form of wild potato.

Food was everywhere, for the taking, if you knew what to look for and how to prepare it, and could adjust the taste to eat it.

A day's travel covered more miles than McCaffey liked to think about, and at night he curled up on the ground and went to sleep, too tired to think about food. The trail they had been following had been faint at best, but the direction had been fairly well established and Tucson was ten miles to the southeast.

But there was no more trail to follow for the raiders began traveling a well-worn road, and their signs were hopelessly blotted by cattlemen and wagons. Cochise was not discouraged or even concerned when they started moving after dawn, and McCaffey had pretty well made up his mind that this was some of Al Gannon's doing, although he had no real proof of it. And this worried him, for he went by the law, even with Al Gannon, and he knew that Cochise wouldn't.

Somehow he'd have to change the Apache's mind.

They camped in the hills near Tucson, and McCaffey began to learn of Apache patience, and of Apache cunning. Neither McCaffey nor Cochise could enter the town, so Yazzi was sent down because adults rarely paid any attention to children.

As the days passed, McCaffey became increasingly restless, but Cochise remained calm and undisturbed, and toward evening on the fifth day, Yazzi returned, wearing a pair of white duck pants and a blue shirt.

"The house of many women gave these to me," he said, explaining to McCaffey, and then to Cochise. He was very proud of his new clothes, and Cochise did not press him or deny him his moment of strutting.

"What did you learn, small warrior?"

Yazzi told his story twice, for McCaffey, and for Cochise: "Much excitement happened to me in the town. A dog bit me. See, he left the marks of his teeth on my leg. It was because of this that the house of women took me in, for I was an object of pity and made many tears flow which was a hard thing for I do not weep. The woman with much fat bought me these clothes with her own money and made me wash myself in a big tub. The woman with much fat was kind to me and gave me a place to sleep, and for this I did much work for her, more work than a man could do. It was not easy for me, but it is the custom of the white man to be ruled by women and to carry the water for them and make the

fires and carry heavy bundles from the store. I was much
liked in the house of women, but at night, when the men
came, I was hidden from them so they would not see me.
But the ears of Yazzi are sharp like the fox and these
eyes did not close in sleep until all the men had gone.
Much talk was heard. There was much laughter and
drinking of *tiswin* and there was fighting among the men
and the woman with much fat would go among them
with a stout stick and hit their heads and make them
yell and run from the house. There was much excitement
every night. Then one night a man came to the house,
and a stillness came over it, for the man walked slowly and
leaned on another man, and he was pale like the stars
and his cheeks were thin from much hunger and one
sleeve of his coat was empty. He became very drunk and
loud and talked of Cochise, and then the other man made
him leave. Later, the other man came back and went into
a room alone with the woman of much fat and they
talked loudly and the man struck the woman and after
he left, she cried. With much courage I showed myself
and she was surprised and told me to keep still about
what I had heard for the man had killed some Apaches
and no one should know about it for much suffering
would come from this deed and there was enough in the
world already. I do not know of this, but the woman of
much fat is wise and speaks much truth. She has a clear
eye that sees much. She cried much and I do not think
it was because the man struck her, for she is strong and
has much courage and is not given to weeping. I believe
she cried because the man had killed children, for the
woman of much fat has a love for children. With her
own hands she made me things in her fire that tasted
sweet and late at night, when the house was still, she
would bring me some of these things in her hand, and a
glass of milk from the cows white men keep. Then she
would talk to me of many things I did not understand
and I do not think she felt it necessary that I understand.
She told me her own life had been one of wickedness and
much wrong, although I do not see it. But she hated the
man with one arm, and the man who struck her, for her

fists would clench when she spoke of them and she would close her eyes and speak to her gods to bring bad medicine upon them. I had heard much to tell you, and I knew I must leave, but kept this from her until I was ready to go, fearing she might want to hold me. She did not. She gave me some of the sweet things for my pocket—see, some crumbs remain for I am weak and ate them. It is with shame that I speak the truth against myself, but it was not easy to leave, and tears were in my eyes as I walked away, taking care that no one would see them. Much excitement happened to me."

Cochise spoke for a minute, then Yazzi said, "He says I did well, Mawcawpee. Do you think so?"

McCaffey squatted before Yazzi and put his hands on his shoulders. "Little man with the ears of the fox, no one could have done better! And soon, when this is over, if Cochise will permit it, I want you to stay with me awhile and my wife will make the sweet things to put in your pocket."

Yazzi asked Cochise, who nodded and spoke. Yazzi beamed and said, "Cochise said that you have much love for me; he can see it in your face and eyes. Is this true, Mawcawpee? He says you would treat me as your own flesh."

"Cochise sees well," McCaffey said. "Ask him what he will do now against the men who killed his people."

This was done and even before the boy translated it, Macaffey knew the answer and was framing an argument. It was not easy, speaking through the boy, but he had his points to make, and he made them, one by one.

"To bring your braves here and kill many people is the wrong thing to do," McCaffey said. "We must be wise, Cochise. And just. We must single out the men who did this bad thing and take them to the army post and try them, and prove them guilty, then hang them."

It wasn't what the Apache wanted; he liked the slow fire and agonized screaming in his ears, and they argued for three hours, gaining little ground on either side.

Finally McCaffey laid his proposition out and drew a line of no retreat. He spoke through Yazzi.

"Hear me clear, Cochise. The world is not governed by Apache law, but the law of the white man. You know me to speak the truth, even in the face of your anger. And I speak the truth now. We will hunt down, you and I and Yazzi, every man who had a part in killing your people. We will drive them to the safety of the fort or take them there and lock them in a building so they cannot escape. When this is done, we will determine their guilt and hang them. If this is not done, we will go separate ways now, and henceforth I will look upon Cochise as a man who is an enemy with no justice in his heart. Decide now, great man. I have waited long enough for your answer."

Cochise hesitated, then spoke at length. The boy repeated his words. "I know Mawcawpee to be a man of his word. I have looked into his eyes when Apache arrows pointed at his heart, and I saw no fear there. Mawcawpee is now a man Cochise would not want for an enemy. It may be as you say, that Apache law does not govern all. Cochise will test your law. We will go your path, Mawcawpee, but if the law is not just, then Cochise will punish for himself."

McCaffey was pleased and offered his hand. "It is our custom, to seal the word of one man to another, a word that can not be broken without dishonor." Cochise took it, then McCaffey spoke of his plan. "We must find the uniforms that were stolen from the soldiers. The man Yazzi spoke of is Al Gannon, and it was his men who pretended to be Apaches when they attacked the soldiers. This man wants war between our people."

"Cochise does not make war unless it is necessary," was the reply.

They left their camp that day and worked away from Tucson, taking a camp in the hills directly in back of the Gannon mine. With what remained of the day they studied the place, the buildings, and the men working, and McCaffey estimated that there must be at least fifty men in Al Gannon's employ.

Tonight, McCaffey thought, would be a good time to go down for a closer look, and he told this to the boy, who relayed it to Cochise. This double conversation was producing some results and McCaffey picked up a few simple words, and added on others. The language, he decided, was not difficult, for everything was expressed in simple terms, without elaboration or structure.

Cochise wanted to wait until near dawn before going down, but McCaffey convinced him that they should not wait that long. Yazzi explained Cochise's reluctance to venture too far away from daylight, for it was a part of his religious belief that a chance death at night would damn him forever. McCaffey then explained that nearly every night some of the men went into Tucson and drank and raised hell, and he didn't want to run into some early riser emptying his kidneys and have the alarm given.

This swayed Cochise and they split the difference, intending to work their way down to the mine buildings halfway between midnight and dawn.

Yazzi was sent out to hunt, and he brought back two rabbits and then found a sheltered spot in the rocks to build a fire and cook them. Afterward they slept and when the night turned cold, McCaffey woke and stirred the boy. Cochise woke, for he seemed to hear the slightest sound, and they left their camp and worked down some poorly defined game trail. McCaffey had long ago stopped worrying about the boy handling himself, for he was strong and quick-witted, and as fleet as a rabbit.

There was only a sliver of a moon, yet the night was clear, and near the main building, two men stood guard, but after watching them for fifteen minutes, McCaffey considered them no problem. In a cavalry company they would not have lasted an hour, for they spent more time standing and talking than they did walking about, and any corporal worth his stripes would have had them in the guardhouse for failure to do their duty properly.

McCaffey didn't think for an instant that he would simply have a look around until he stumbled onto something; a man could find too much trouble that way. He'd tried to put himself into Al Gannon's place, figuring that since getting the uniforms had taken some brutal doing, they would be kept for future use, if the Indians needed a further prod along the warpath.

He's got them safely hidden, McCaffey concluded, and he knew that only a few of Gannon's men knew about the uniforms; he wouldn't trust such knowledge to all his men. That rather limited the hiding place, for it would have to be somewhere that only a few men ever went. Not the mine shaft, or the equipment shed, or even the main office building. That left the bunkhouses, the cook shack, and the powdershed.

The powdershed was McCaffey's choice, but it was behind the main building and the two guards blocked his way. He made a circling motion with his hand and they skirted around, coming in from the other side so that their approach was hidden from the two guards.

A stout lock on the powdershed door made McCaffey wonder how he was going to get in, then he motioned for Cochise and Yazzi to stay hidden and moved toward the rear of the main building. He tried several windows before he found one that moved under his hand, and he opened it and pulled himself inside. The odors told him that he was in the assayer's office, and he moved slowly and carefully so as not to stumble or knock anything over and make a noise.

He emerged into a short hallway and stopped, finding it dark and deserted. Then he moved along, opening doors and closing them until he came to what was apparently Al Gannon's office. Quietly he eased in and went to the desk and went through the drawers, feeling carefully, yet trying not to visibly disturb the contents. He found several keys, but not the one he wanted; they were too small for the massive lock on the powdershed door.

His search turned up nothing, so he thought about it and the more he thought, the more convinced he became that the key was somewhere around; it would be too bulky for a man to carry in his pocket. His hand probed carefully the underside of the desk, and far in back he found a small nail with a key hanging from it. The size of it convinced him, and he let himself out the way he had entered.

The key fit the lock perfectly and they stepped into the powdershed, leaving Yazzi to guard the door. The darkness was a thick blanket and McCaffey searched by feel; he knew what he was looking for, wooden crates with US Army burned into the sides.

His fingers passed over kegs and small boxes, and then he found his prize. He tapped Cochise and they went to the door; McCaffey carefully locked it, then ducked away before Cochise could stop him.

He wanted to put that key back on the nail and get out in a hurry, for his plan was now fully formed, and he needed the element of complete surprise if it was to work.

14

CAPTAIN LOVERING was sleeping when the orderly came to his quarters and knocked on the door. He got up, trying not to disturb his wife, but was unsuccessful. A dawn light was beginning to break and she sat up in bed.

"Go back to sleep," he said and left the bedroom and went to the door.

"Sorry to bother you, sir, but an Indian boy came on the post. He has a message for you. Most unusual, sir."

"I'll meet you in my office in ten minutes," Lovering said and went back for his shirt and boots. The officer of the day and sergeant of the guard were both in his office. Yazzi stood with a paper clenched in his hand, a bit frightened but trying not to show it.

"Well, what have we here?" Lovering asked. He took the paper and turned to the lamp and read it twice. Then he looked at the Indian boy, but spoke to the sergeant of the guard. "See that he's taken to the mess hall and given a good meal, then have the bugler blow assembly."

The sergeant and the boy went out and Lovering turned the OD to the wall map. "McCaffey says he'll be in this locality waiting for us. Now I don't pretend to understand the whole of this; the note is written on Gannon's stationery, but it's unmistakably McCaffey's writing. He says that he has found the stolen uniforms, but will need a full company of cavalry to recover them."

The bugler was sounding his horn as Lovering ran across the grounds to his quarters. His wife was up now; he brushed past her to get his pistol belt and put some spare cigars in his pocket.

He told her what all soldiers tell their wives; that he'd be back when he got there and not to worry, then he ran out and met his sergeant by headquarters.

Before the edge of the sun showed, the company, with Lovering commanding, rode off the post and away from Tucson. They were not a mile away when the sergeant sided Lovering and pointed back, and the company was stopped. Yazzi, afoot and running for all his worth, was trying to catch up.

"Go back and pick him up, sergeant," Lovering said. They waited and finally the sergeant returned and Lovering fixed a stern eye on the boy. "Why are you following us? This is no place for boys."

"I am a man. Cochise himself has said this. I go to be with Mawcawpee."

The sergeant said, "He can ride double with me, sir."

"Very well," Lovering said. "We can't waste time talking about it." He waved the company into motion again.

He followed a long, circuitous route for nearly two hours, working higher into the hills, moving through narrow canyons and dry washes until he came to a high valley. Then he raised his hand quickly and halted the company for Cochise and Linus McCaffey emerged from the rocks where they'd been hiding. Lovering swung down and ordered his troop to do so and McCaffey lifted Yazzi off the sergeant's horse and hugged him.

"I knew you would not fail, little warrior." He set him down and shook Lovering's hand. McCaffey's face was whiskered and he was incredibly dirty and thinner in body, yet he somehow seemed stronger, more positive. "Sorry I couldn't explain more fully, sir, but I only had that one piece of paper I filched from Al Gannon's office. You can make cook fires here. We're pretty sheltered." He turned then to Cochise, and motioned him forward. "Captain, I want you to meet the Apache leader, Cochise. We've been on a little scouting expedition together."

"Obviously not near water," Lovering said, standing back a pace. Then he laughed. "I didn't bring a razor, or I'd loan it to you. Where are the uniforms?"

"In the powdershed at Gannon's mine," McCaffey said. He explained how he had taken the key from Gannon's office, and scouted the powdershed.

Lovering said, "That was a bit of gall. Suppose Gannon's moved them?"

"I doubt that, sir. He likely doesn't suspect that we were there at all, because I put the key back."

"Good Lord," Lovering said. "When do you suggest that we move, Mr. McCaffey?"

"I think, sir, that a routine, casual entrance would be most effective, and Gannon would only be annoyed without suspecting your exact purpose. At the right time, Cochise and I will appear and I'll get the key and then we'll have a look."

"It rather appeals to my sense of the dramatic," Lovering said. "Of course, Gannon will put up a fight."

"Perhaps, but not if we deploy properly." The sergeant came over with a cup of coffee and McCaffey sniffed it. "I've been living on rats and rattlesnakes and rabbits; this smells too good to drink." He explained to Lovering the bargain he had made with Cochise on the capture and punishment of the men who killed the Apache women, and as he talked he knew that he had exceeded his authority, but Lovering sensibly did not question it, or retreat from the position McCaffey had put him in.

"That Indian boy has formed an attachment to you," Lovering said. "Saying goodbye to him won't be easy."

"I haven't said goodbye yet," McCaffey said.

Lovering decided that it was time to move on, and he rode out while McCaffey and Cochise remained behind. Yazzi slept in the shade of a rock. When McCaffey woke him, they moved afoot along the ridge and in the early afternoon they paused above the mine and saw Lovering and his troop approach.

They dismounted in the main yard near the central building and Al Gannon came out. McCaffey looked at Cochise; the Apache nodded and they started down, working their way among the rocks.

It took them forty minutes to reach the mine. Lovering

had made no attempt to conduct a search; he seemed bent on a purely social call for he and Gannon stood on the porch of the main building.

Gannon saw them approach and shouted something to one of his men, but a soldier blocked the move toward a weapon, and McCaffey paused with his foot on the bottom step.

"I thought you were going to leave the country, Al."

"I'm making plans," Gannon said. He looked at Cochise and the boy. "What is this?" He glanced at Captain Lovering. "Ain't you going to arrest this Indian?"

"No," Lovering said. "I think I'll arrest you for the murder of the quartermaster guard, three teamsters, and the stealing of government property."

"You're crazy," Al Gannon said.

"Excuse me," McCaffey said and brushed past him and went in and got the key from under the desk. He came back and held it up and said, "Shall I tell you where I got this, Al?" He tossed it to the sergeant. "Take a detail and open the powdershed. You'll find the loot there."

There was no way for Al Gannon to escape the trap, yet the compulsion was stronger than he could resist; he bolted off the porch, past McCaffey and Cochise before they could stop him, but Yazzi dropped to his knees and Gannon tripped over him.

Like a cat, Cochise was on him, knife at his throat, and McCaffey said, "You have given me your word, Cochise!"

The point of the knife touched Al Gannon's throat hard enough to draw a drop of blood, but it pressed no further; Cochise hauled him to his feet and two soldiers made Gannon a prisoner.

Systematically the miners were rounded up and held in an area by the cookshack, and the stolen government property was taken from the powdershed and stacked in the yard to be counted. Cochise watched this for a time, then spoke through the boy.

"Many men stood on the ridge in the soldier clothes, Mawcawpee. Yet there is only one man taken prisoner."

"I have given you my word," McCaffey said. "All the

men who were there will be caught." He turned to Lovering. "May I suggest, sir, that the entire work force here be placed under arrest until their whereabouts can be established."

"We have no stockade big enough to hold them," Lovering said. "However we might set up a temporary prisoner-of-war camp." He frowned. "I would like to point out that these men are not without recourse to law. Unless we establish the actual members of the raiding party, we will have to turn them loose or face some sticky litigation."

"Captain, would you say that we had two days?"

"I wouldn't recommend holding them longer," Lovering said. "There's a question in mind now as to whether this is a military or legal matter. Indian affairs are properly the jurisdiction of a U. S. marshal. Unfortunately the nearest is in Prescott."

"Then we could properly hold them until the marshal arrived," McCaffey said. "That would provide us with enough time to secure several witnesses who could see the merit of a confession."

"I'm beginning to see your point," Lovering said. "What do you suggest?"

"I'd like to select two men and have them turned loose," McCaffey said. "Of course it ought to be done properly, without Gannon or anyone in his crew knowing about it. Cochise and I will take it from there."

"Define that," Lovering invited.

"Well, sir, I don't think we could really convict Al Gannon or anyone else without a confession, names and all that. Cochise and I will get that from the two men you release."

"Apache torture, Mr. McCaffey?"

"No, sir, but certainly the threat of it. Captain, we're not playing a game by the rules. Gannon is a vicious man. He's got to be killed or locked up for good. And I'm sorry I didn't shoot him when I had the chance. Dan Gannon is up and around now; you'd best expect all kinds of trouble from him."

"Can he be fool enough to think he can buck the army?" Lovering said.

"Sir, the Gannons have had things their own way for so long that they have no regard for anyone's law. They are like wound clocks, sir, destined to run until broken."

"We must be careful how we break them then. Or we won't have much of a career to look forward to. Mr. McCaffey, the crusader for peace and justice must guard that he does not become as the men he seeks to destroy. We'll settle this in a court, Mr. McCaffey. Make no bones about that."

"That's what I told Cochise," McCaffey said. "If some word could be given my wife that I'm all right—"

"I'll send her my personal report," Lovering said. "It might be best if I held the prisoners here. This evening, I'll begin the questioning, and toward dawn, I'll turn two of the tough ones loose. Be watching for them." He turned his head and looked toward the town road where a spiral of dust rose. Then a buggy came around the bend and Dan Gannon halted in the yard. He dismounted and walked slowly toward Lovering, a gaunt, worn man with an empty sleeve tucked into his coat pocket. For a moment he failed to recognize McCaffey behind the whiskers, then his eyes turned flat and dead of expression.

"The army in the mining business now?" Dan Gannon asked. He saw his brother standing some distance away, flanked by armed troopers. "Turn him loose!"

"It's not quite that easy," Lovering said. "Al Gannon had some stolen government property here. He's under arrest."

"Looks like I'm going to have to get a lawyer," Dan Gannon said. He glanced at McCaffey. "Your idea?"

"Now that you mention it, yes."

"You've been trouble to me since I first saw you," Dan Gannon declared. "Why ain't you dead?"

"Probably because you aren't man enough to kill me," McCaffey pointed out. "You and your brother have had enough chances, but you were bound sooner or later to run into something you couldn't handle. So you get a lawyer. Get a good one."

"That's the only kind I know," Dan Gannon said.

"The charge," Paul Lovering said, "is murder. And if I can't prove your brother killed the quartermaster guards, I'll prove they fired into the Apache village and killed innocent women and children."

"You'll have a hell of a time getting a conviction," Gannon said. "You've got witnesses?"

"Two," McCaffey said, smiling. "Does that worry you?"

"Not a bit," Gannon said. "I don't know a thing about it."

"Of course not," McCaffey said. "That's why you got drunk at Bessie's place and shot your mouth off. Afterwards you came back and threatened her and hit her."

If he'd struck Dan Gannon McCaffey could not have produced a more surprised reaction. "Why that fat old—" He clamped his teeth together and stood that way for a minute. Then he thought about it and relaxed. "So what did she tell you? I heard about it in town, that's all. You'll have a hell of a time proving that I didn't."

"You didn't hear a thing in town," McCaffey said. "I know that because the Apaches secretly buried their dead. They told no one, so you heard no rumors, Dan. You heard it from the men who stood on the ridge and fired into the Apache camp."

"I wasn't there."

"No, you weren't," Lovering said. "But you know all about it, Gannon. You could give us names. You could tell what you know."

"You'll wait a long time for that," Dan Gannon said, and turned to his buggy.

When he drove out, Lovering said, "I'd better put a guard outside Bessie's place. He might try to kill her."

"He couldn't be that stupid," McCaffey said.

"Would you like to bet Bessie's life on it?"

"No," McCaffey said. "If you can spare some rations, we'll go back to the hills."

Lovering smiled. "I thought you were doing well on rats and rattlesnakes?"

"I like to vary my diet, sir, that's all."

15

AT MCCAFFEY'S REQUEST, Captain Lovering sent the sergeant into town to make a few purchases, and when he came back, he gave McCaffey a small paper bag and they left the mine and returned to a hill camp. Cochise had a fondness for coffee and as soon as they made a small fire, McCaffey put on his small tin pot and brewed some.

While he and Cochise shared the coffee, McCaffey motioned for Yazzi to come over. He said, "Have you ever eaten candy?"

The boy shook his head and Cochise looked at McCaffey and waited. Offering the paper sack, Yazzi dipped his hand in and took two pieces, then hesitated and put one back. He sucked the lemon drop for a moment, then he smiled.

"It is a goodness I have never tasted before," he said.

"The whole sack is yours," McCaffey said.

The boy took it solemnly and said, "I will be strong and eat only a piece each day and it will last a long time, Mawcawpee."

Cochise spoke at length, then Yazzi translated.

"He asks, did you send the soldier to town just to buy these sweet things for me?" McCaffey nodded and Cochise spoke again. "He says you are a man with much heart to think of a small boy."

The Apache elected to stand guard while McCaffey and the boy slept, and later, McCaffey woke and spent the cold, silent hours of the night crouched on a rock, looking down on the lamplit mine buildings.

Dawn came, an advancing grayness, and finally McCaffey could make out some movement in the yard. Two horses were brought up and two men rode out together and they followed the canyon a way before splitting up.

Cochise spoke and Yazzi said, "He will follow the one on the roan horse. We will follow the one on the bay."

"Tell him I will meet him in Tucson," McCaffey said and turned away with the boy. They started back along the ridge, making for the high pass some miles beyond where the canyon ended and gave the rider a clear shot to the Prescott road.

With luck, MacCaffey believed, he could head the man off and take him by surprise. It would be fast traveling for a man afoot, but he was tough and getting tougher by the day and he had learned how to travel from Cochise. An Apache didn't walk; he jogged along, taking big, loose steps that was near a slow run, and he always kept the knees springy and moved on the balls of his feet. It was that blasted stamping along, infantry-style, that gave a man blisters.

They moved through the heat of the day; the sweat rolled down McCaffey's face, soaked his shirt and evaporated quickly with a cooling effect. He knew that he was almost at the summit of the pass and slowed his pace, picking carefully a spot from where he could command a view of the trail. Further down, moving along, came the lone rider.

He motioned the boy to dash across and hide on the other side, then drew his pistol and waited.

The rider came on, moving as rapidly as caution would allow; he was armed with a pistol and a Sharps rifle, and McCaffey wondered how he would take this man without a lot of shooting. He figured that the man would try to get off a shot with the rifle, and if he did, he'd go for his pistol without stopping to reload the Sharps.

I'll have to get him then, McCaffey decided. His intention was to let the man get slightly past then take him from behind, but it just didn't work out that way. The rider was almost abreast when he halted at some suspicious thing, some inner sense warning him, and McCaffey knew he couldn't wait any longer. Each second lost sharpened the man's awareness, so he pounced from his hiding place and threw down on him with his revolver.

"Reach high!"

The man fired the Sharps hurriedly and the bullet whanged off a rock, then he wheeled his horse and would have broken free had not Yazzi thrown a rock and struck the animal on the neck. The frightened horse reared and unseated the rider just as he fired his revolver at the boy. Yazzi cried out and rolled on the ground, clutching the calf of his leg.

McCaffey had no choice now; he dropped the hammer on his Remington and saw the man flung back by the bullet. Wounded, McCaffey felt that he could wrest the gun away from the man and jumped on him, but there was more strength left in the downed man than he had reckoned with. In spite of his wounded arm, the man put up a stiff fight, and they rolled about, struggling to take possession of the gun. McCaffey wanted to disarm the man while the man wanted to bring the weapon into play. Then McCaffey managed to get the man's good arm twisted behind him and he thought he had it done, but the gun went off and the man fell limp, the bullet passing into his back just under the shoulder blades.

He died there, coughing blood and kicking up dust with his boots, and McCaffey turned to the boy, who had braced himself against a rock, and tried with his hands to stop the bleeding in his leg.

Tearing part of his pants leg, McCaffey bound the wound; it looked fierce, for the bullet had gone through the muscle and the bleeding was bad. The bandage helped staunch the flow of blood and he caught up the dead man's horse, led him back, and lifted the boy to the saddle. Then he mounted and started back, hoping that Cochise would have better luck.

He tried to hurry, yet ease the boy's pain, and he was not at all successful either way. By the time he sighted the mine buildings, the sun was well down and when he rode into the yard, Lovering hurried forward and took the boy down from the horse.

"Sergeant! Bring the first aid packet. Corporal, hitch up a wagon and throw some hay in it. We'll take the boy to town and let Dr. Caswell have a look at him." His glance touched McCaffey. "No luck, huh?"

"There was a lot of shooting," McCaffey said. "Sorry, sir, but Cochise may have better luck."

"Well, I picked two men who howled loudest about being innocent, figuring they were the guiltiest. So don't lose any sleep over this."

"No, sir, but I want to get the job done. Making peace with the Indians is going to be difficult enough without someone stirring them up."

"It's history, all down the line," Lovering said. "Peace on one hand and warmaking with the Indians on the other. If a man was to bet that the Pilgrims, six months after they landed, were working on ways to get rid of the Indians, he'd have a sure thing."

"Is Al Gannon still here or did you move him in town?"

"We've got him locked up and two soldiers guarding the door," Lovering said. "Why don't you go on into town with the boy. Get a shave and a bath and a hot meal and sleep in the hotel tonight."

"That sounds good," McCaffey said. "My wife—"

"The dispatch rider ought to be there by now." Lovering smiled. "Linus, if we fail, it's nothing personal."

"Isn't it, sir?"

When the wagon came up, he got in back with Yazzi, who was stretched out on some tossed hay. The boy said, "Am I not brave, Mawcawpee? Not a tear has come to my eyes."

"You are a brave soldier," McCaffey said and held the boy's head in his lap all the way to town.

Doctor Caswell was not in his office, but the sergeant went to get him and he came in fifteen minutes later and immediately examined the boy's leg. "Not too serious," he said. "A good deal of tissue damage, though. Well, we'll fix you right up, young fella. In a couple of weeks you'll be feeling fine."

He bathed the wound, cleaned it, probed it for any

foreign matter, and was bandaging it when Dan Gannon came in. His face was thin and he seemed to shiver from some inner cold. Caswell excused himself and took him into another room and remained there with him for five minutes. Then Gannon went out another door and Caswell came back.

"Twice a day," he said to McCaffey. "Next month it will be three times a day, then four. He hasn't got long the way he's going. Amputations are bad business. Only the strong survive."

"I always thought he was strong," McCaffey said.

"Inner strength is what I'm talking about," Caswell said. "You don't have to stick around if you don't want to. I'll give the boy something to make him sleep and ease the pain. Come back later this evening."

"All right," McCaffey said. He patted Yazzi on the head. "I'll bring you some more lemon drops."

"It is with shame that I dropped them," Yazzi said. "So great a gift must not be treated lightly."

McCaffey went out, but waited for Caswell and finally the doctor came out and closed the door. "They're all brave," he said. "Don't know what fear is. Someday, when he's grown, he'll be looking down a gun barrel at some soldier and then he won't think about lemon drops."

"That's not a pretty picture."

"Probably accurate though," Caswell said. "How come you're towing him around, lieutenant?"

"A long story," McCaffey said.

"All right, it's none of my business. You like the boy. Better cut that out. One of these days you'll have to send him back to his people and it won't be easy."

"Why do I have to do that?"

"Because he's Apache."

McCaffey shook his head. "He's Pima."

"But raised Apache." He smiled. "Think of your wife, man. She's a lot of woman, but she couldn't take that."

"She wouldn't bat an eye," McCaffey said. "Eloise is all iron."

He left the doctor's office and went to the barber shop

where he bought a bath and a shave, then went to the hotel and got a room.

The bed felt strange to him after so many nights on the bare ground, but he stretched out and started to doze. In the adjoining room, a man swore and cried and threw things, but finally he quieted down and McCaffey went to sleep.

It was fully dark when he woke, got up and washed his face, then went down to a restaurant to get something to eat. The street was full of activity and a group of soldiers were laughing in front of the saloon; they all went inside and it set McCaffey to thinking about a glass of beer.

Later, he decided and went on to the restaurant. Afterward he went to Caswell's place to see Yazzi, but the boy was still asleep and Caswell didn't think it wise to wake him. McCaffey returned to the hotel and let himself into his room and found Captain Lovering there.

From the expression on Lovering's face, McCaffey knew that Cochise had returned. "Well, sir?" McCaffey said.

"The man is dead," Lovering said. "No, Cochise didn't kill him. He surprised him, as near as I can tell and the man wheeled his horse, fell off a narrow trail and rolled nearly to the bottom of the canyon. Cochise brought him back. A bag of broken bones."

"So we're back where we started," McCaffey said, discouragement in his voice.

"Not exactly," Lovering pointed out. "We've still got Bessie. I'm sure she'll cooperate and tell what she knows. It may be enough to tie Al and Dan Gannon into the Apache killings. Linus, I don't really care on what charge they hang. Just as long as they stretch rope."

"Do you still have the guard around Bessie's place?"

"Hell yes. Four men are at all sides of the building." He took out a cigar and lit it. "I haven't had a chance to talk to Bessie to find out what she really knows. Do you think the Indian boy was giving it to you straight?"

"Lying?" McCaffey shook his head. "Yazzi wouldn't know what a lie was. No, Dan got drunk in Bessie's place and shot off his mouth. And knowing him, he must have shot it off plenty."

"We'll get Bessie's statement in the morning." He smiled. "I wouldn't like to interrupt the flow of her business tonight. It might make her uncooperative." He got up and clamped his cigar between his teeth. "Feel like a glass of beer and some cards?"

"All right," McCaffey said. They left the room and paused in the hall while McCaffey locked his door. In the room next to his, McCaffey saw the strong streak of lamplight from beneath the door. And as he walked down the hall with Lovering, he said, "A real wild man lives in there. Before I went to sleep he was cussing and throwing things."

"There's all kinds in this town."

The saloon was a busy place and they found a table and took their beer there. Soldiers crowded against the bar, edging civilians away just to be doing it, and McCaffey could understand why they were unpopular wherever they went. He supposed it was the uniform, making one man pretty much like another, giving them a feeling of strength that civilians didn't have.

It never bothered him in that way because he was an officer and he lived a life completely removed from this. Lovering said, "You're looking serious, Linus."

"Was I?" He brightened. "Maybe it was the long stretch of service ahead of me that was getting me down. A man looks back and two years seems like a long time, but then he looks ahead and the next thirty seem like an eternity."

Dan Gannon came in, bought a drink, had his look around, then went out. Lovering said, "He reminds me of a chicken hawk looking for a full henhouse."

"Maybe I ought to see what he's up to," McCaffey said and started to rise. But Lovering put out his hand and pushed him back.

"Enjoy your beer, Linus. Don't try to do it all."

16

STANDING BEHIND THE THIN WALL of his hotel room, Dan Gannon heard clearly everything Captain Lovering and Linus McCaffey said, and after he heard them go on down the hall, Gannon let himself out quietly and went to the lobby. The clerk was busy at the desk, and he turned back, exiting by the back door.

He knew every dark street, every gap between buildings in which to pause while a horseman or stroller passed by, and then he would go on, working his way toward Bessie's place. The soldiers were on duty, and he stood in the dark shadow of the barn near the vacant lot, the barn in which Mike Shotten had hidden after the gun fight, and it brought a bitter gall of memory to Dan Gannon.

To get into Bessie's place without being seen would take some doing, and he wondered how he was going to do it. Then he figured that nothing drew a crowd like a fire; even the soldiers would be pulled away from their post by it, and he went into the barn, found some hay, and put a match to it. He got away before the fire shed too much light and was crouched near the ground when the soldiers saw the blaze and sounded the alarm.

Men and girls poured out of Bessie's place, and Gannon went in through an open back window. He knew where he was and opened slowly the door leading into the hall and then quickly made his way toward Bessie's quarters. There was a light coming from beneath the door and he heard her stirring in there and eased it open. She was sitting at the table, a bottle and glass nearby, an old newspaper propped up in front of her. Some sound must have alerted her, for she slowly turned her head and looked at him, no surprise at all on her face.

"I've been expecting you, Dan. I figured the fire was your doing."

"You should have run like hell," Gannon said.

"Too fat," Bessie said. "Besides, I'm not afraid of you now."

Gannon frowned and put his hand on the butt of his pistol. "Don't you know what I'm going to do?"

"I know," Bessie said. "But it won't do you any good."

"You fat old bitch," Gannon said and pulled his gun, firing as it came hip high. Bessie flinched when the bullet hit her, and then she slowly fell out of her chair. The house seemed to shake when she hit the floor, and Gannon wheeled and dashed out and down the hall.

Before he went out the window he paused and heard no alarm being spread for the yelling near the fire had completely drowned out the sound of the shot. Quickly he dropped to the ground and made his way back to the hotel, locking the back door from the inside before going on to his room. He cleaned his pistol and then stretched out on the bed and went to sleep.

One of the girls found Bessie and screamed, which brought the others and nearly every customer in the place on the run. Bessie was growing cold and someone went for the doctor, and he came, along with Captain Lovering and Linus McCaffey.

"She's been dead nearly three hours," Caswell said, completing his examination. He stood up and sniffed and took off his glasses to wipe his eyes.

Lovering turned to those crowded into the hall. "Who found her?"

One of the girls raised her hand.

"She was dead for some time," McCaffey said. "Doesn't anyone come in here?"

"We don't bother Bessie," the girl said. "Not unless there's trouble."

"Was there trouble?" Lovering asked.

"Well, no," the girl said. "I wasn't feeling good and I

wanted to go to bed. It's something I had to ask Bessie about."

Caswell said, "Three hours. Mmmm, that would put it about the time of the fire."

"Mr. McCaffey," Lovering said. "Have the sergeant arrest the men on duty here."

"Yes, sir." He went out and Caswell motioned for the others to go on about their business. McCaffey came back and closed the door.

"She was a fat old woman who knew more sin than all of us put together, but I admired her," Caswell said. "There wasn't a lie in her, or a deceitful bone in her body." He looked at Lovering. "Can you tell me why this happened?"

"She had to be shut up," Lovering said softly. "She didn't know much and I doubt whether it would have stood up in court, but it was enough to scare the Gannons."

"Al couldn't have done this," McCaffey said. "He's locked up at the mine along with his toughs."

"We'll have to check that," Lovering said. "In the meantime, we'll look in on Dan Gannon."

"He's at the hotel," Caswell said. He took Lovering's arm. "Captain, I've seen men killed and it's bothered me, but Bessie was wasted. You know what I mean?"

"She won't be wasted, doctor," Lovering said. "Arizona has had enough of men like the Gannons. Let's go to the hotel."

"I'll stay here," Caswell said.

Lovering and McCaffey left the house and walked down the dark street. Finally McCaffey said, "Sir, what can we really do with Dan Gannon except ask him questions?"

"Nothing," Lovering said. "But we'll ask them anyway."

The clerk woke when they came in and circled his desk to see who was going upstairs. McCaffey turned to the man and said, "Mind your own business now," and his tone of voice was convincing enough to show that he meant it.

At Gannon's door, Lovering knocked and Gannon grumbled something and Lovering knocked again. "What the hell you want? Who is it?"

"Captain Lovering. Open the door."

"Go to hell," Gannon said. "Let me sleep."

Lovering backed up, raised his foot, and drove it through the panel. He reached inside, pulled the bolt and flung it open. Gannon was turning up his bed lamp and blinking. His pistol lay on a chair near his bed and McCaffey picked it up, sniffed the barrel, then slipped it back into the holster.

"Now what the hell is this?" Gannon asked. "You know, this ain't right, bustin' into a man's room while he's sleepin'. I could have shot both of you and got away with it."

"You wouldn't have gotten away with it," McCaffey said evenly. "I'd have blown your brains out."

"Soldier, you've had it in for me since we first met." He shook his head. "Tell me what you want and get the hell out."

"I suppose you haven't left this room?"

"Not since supper I ain't," Dan said.

"Can you prove that?" Lovering asked.

"Do I have to?"

"Don't get smart," McCaffey advised.

Gannon shrugged. "I don't know. Ask the clerk."

"We will," Lovering said. He turned to the door and waited, then McCaffey joined him and they went down the hall.

"His gun was clean," McCaffey said.

"He could have cleaned it." Lovering shook his head. "I don't think we could prove anything on him." They went out to the street and stood on the porch. The town was quiet and few lights burned. "Bessie could have talked and it might have scared one of Gannon's men into a confession. That was my hope, but it's gone now. We might as well turn Al and his men loose and start all over."

"A miserable thought, sir."

"Hell, the whole thing's miserable. A man starts out to

build a string of army posts and ends up cleaning out the lawless elements before he can get halfway started." He blew out a long breath. "Let's get some sleep. We may get a fresh slant on it in the daylight."

Lovering mounted and rode out of town, heading for the mine. McCaffey remained standing on the porch for a time, then he sat down in a chair and cocked his feet to the rail, enjoying the quiet and the cool night air. Doctor Caswell came down the street, his step slow and plodding and he saw McCaffey there and stopped.

He sat down and put his bag on the porch. "This is a day I could have skipped," Caswell said. He looked at McCaffey. "Did you talk to Dan?"

"He said he's been in bed all evening."

"The lying bastard," Caswell said. "Who else could have pulled the trigger?"

"He could have paid to have it done," McCaffey said.

"Yes, but he'll tell me," Caswell said. He smiled when McCaffey stared. "That's right, he'll tell me. He'll beg to tell me everything. If you want a confession, you bring the captain around to Dan's hotel room around four in the afternoon. He'll talk then."

"What are you thinking of doing?"

"Violating my oath," Caswell said and went into the hotel.

Gannon was trying to fix the lock on his door when Caswell pushed it open and stepped into the room. He looked at Gannon and said, "Had a busy night, didn't you?"

"What does that mean?"

Caswell shrugged. "I saw the army leave. Dan, you shouldn't have shot Bessie."

Gannon laughed. "Are you going to start that too?"

"Yes, and I guess I'll finish it," Caswell said. "You're going to tell me all about it, Dan."

He stared, then laughed again. "You've lost your mind."

"We'll see," Caswell said. He walked over to the chair near Gannon's bed, took the pistol from the holster, then threw it through the window without bothering to open it.

"What the hell's the idea of that?" Gannon snapped. "Get out of here!" He made an advance toward Caswell, who waited until he got close enough, then knocked Gannon flat.

While the man was still on the floor, Caswell said, "I can lick you, Dan. You're not strong enough to fight me. So we'll just wait until you're ready to tell me all about it."

"You've got a damned long wait coming," Gannon said and stretched out on the bed.

Caswell glanced at his watch. "About twelve hours, I'd say, and I don't mind waiting."

"Wait then," Gannon said and fell asleep.

Caswell sat in his chair and watched Gannon, and before dawn the man began to stir restlessly, and finally woke, a film of sweat on his face. He got up and paced around the room and complained of pain in his stump, but Caswell told him that it would pass.

When it was fully daylight, Gannon wanted something to eat so Caswell thumped the floor for the clerk and ordered a breakfast, but when it came, it turned Gannon's stomach and he couldn't eat any of it.

McCaffey came soon afterward and he looked at Dan Gannon, then at Fred Caswell. Gannon's hand was trembling and he sweat a great deal although the day had not begun to turn off hot.

"Is he sick?" McCaffey asked.

"Yes," Caswell calmly. "He needs his narcotics, and he isn't going to get it." He looked at Dan Gannon and smiled. "Do you understand what's the matter with you? All the narcotics you took to kill the pain of the amputation have caused you to become addicted to the drug. To stop taking them now will be like going to hell and back, if you're man enough to make it."

"Lovering's got one arm and he's not—"

Caswell silenced McCaffey. "Lovering lost his early in the war and he endured the agony because the surgeons wouldn't give him the laudanum. Then too, we're speaking of a different breed of man, lieutenant. When I'm speaking of Gannon, I'm not really speaking of a man at all."

"You son of a bitch," Gannon said and started toward Caswell, but stopped.

"He lacks the guts to attack me now," Caswell said. "You'd better get out of here. In three hours he'll be turned into a raving maniac. I think I'm best equipped to handle him."

"I don't want to see it," McCaffey said, and went out.

He met Lovering as the man rode into town and they had breakfast together and McCaffey told him what Caswell was doing. Lovering's face turned bleak, but he made no offer to stop Caswell.

"It may be the only way," he said. "God, I feel for the man, no good though he is. I had trouble along that line myself, although the surgeons gave me very little to kill the pain. A man thinks he'll die, then fears that he won't, to end it all." He sat for a moment in silence. "My dear wife was sworn on a Bible by me to lock me in a room and not to let me out for a week. I tell you, Linus, I put fingernail grooves in the plaster of the walls before I beat the devilish habit. A man will rave out of his mind and grow sick and be racked with the pain of cramps before he rids his system of the effects. And it takes damned little to get a man started."

McCaffey took out his watch. "Caswell said we should come to the room at four o'clock."

Lovering nodded. "He'll be approaching what he thinks is the worst then, but it'll only be the beginning." He pushed his breakfast away unfinished. "I'm expecting a dispatch rider today. Perhaps there'll be something there from your wife. A man can stand a cheery note in this business."

"Where is Cochise?"

"At the mine," Lovering said. "He asked about the boy. Is he his son?"

McCaffey shook his head. "I don't think he has anyone. Captain, what would the army say if an officer took him to raise?"

"I had a notion you'd bring that up. Better talk it over with your wife, Linus."

"Someday, someone has to take that step, sir."

"Yes, they'll have to accept our ways, and to do that, they'll have to live with us," Lovering said. "Mr. Mc-Caffey, I wouldn't recommend that you pioneer this field. But then I know I'm talking to deaf ears." He got up and laid fifty cents on the table. "Send someone to the mine for me before four o'clock."

17

MIKE SHOTTEN came to town in the early afternoon, parked his wagon along the crowded street, and turned his head toward the hotel, where everyone's attention was directed. It sounded as though someone was ripping partitions out of an upstairs room. Shotten got down from the wagon as McCaffey came up and the two men shook hands briefly.

"Got a letter here from your wife," Shotten said, and handed it over. "What's going on?" He jerked his thumb toward the hotel.

"Doc Caswell's getting Dan Gannon to swear off morphine," McCaffey said. "I don't know how long my nerves can go on standing the yelling and howling." He took Shotten by the arm. "Let me buy you a drink."

They went into the saloon and Shotten ordered, then said, "Go on, read your letter. I'll put this down slow and order another."

McCaffey smiled his thanks and turned away. He opened the envelope and read:

My Dearest Linus:
In spite of my fears, I knew you would be safe; I prayed for you and knew my prayers were not unheard. The weather has been beastly hot and some of my dishes were broken on the way here, and I packed them so carefully. Lieutenant Saunders' wife arrived. It's good to have company. Know that I love you and miss you.

Eloise

McCaffey folded the letter and turned back to the bar.

Shotten said, "It's good to have a woman. Want a drink? I guess I'll have another. If I drink enough I might stop thinking about Dan Gannon." He motioned the bartender over, had his glass filled, and tossed it off, then coughed and wiped his watering eyes. "Noonan's a few hours behind me, escorting two more wagons. He worried about you, Linus."

"Has he stayed sober?"

"Cold sober," Shotten said. He looked past McCaffey as the clerk came into the saloon. He saw McCaffey and motioned for him and both men left the bar.

"Doc wants you right away. And the captain too."

"The captain's at the mine," McCaffey said. "Send someone out there. And tell them to hurry it up." He hurried across the street and elbowed his way through the men blocking the hotel entrance. Shotten followed him down the hall and McCaffey knocked on Gannon's door.

Caswell let them in and he looked like a man who had fought valiantly to win. His coat was torn and there was a bruise on his face and his glasses had been broken. Dan Gannon sat on the floor, his knees drawn up tight against his chest, and what clothing he wore was torn, ripped by his own hand in the agony of his withdrawal from the drug. His fist was bloody and there were smudges of blood on the walls where he had struck them. He seemed to be nearer death than life and trembled violently.

Caswell said, "He's ready to talk now."

Shotten said, "This hardly seems human."

Whirling on him, Caswell snapped, "This is a medical matter, between a doctor and his patient. Now don't make anything else of it."

"Just a remark," Shotten said.

Caswell took a pitcher of water and poured it over Gannon's head, then said, "Answer me now. Who held up the army wagons and stole the uniforms?"

"Al did." He spoke with chattering teeth. "God help me!"

In a glass of water, Caswell mixed a powder and Gannon began to crawl toward him but Caswell kicked him away. "Tell me more. Who killed the Apaches?"

"Al! Al! Al!"

"More names."

Gannon sobbed and beat his hand on the floor. "Keating. Jacoby. Sessions was there too." He shook his head. "That's all I know for sure."

Caswell looked at McCaffey and Shotten. "You're witness to this confession. Confronting those four ought to get them to name the others." He handed the glass to Gannon who had to be helped or he would have spilled it. After he drank it, he fell back on the floor and coughed and drew painfully for air. "We can go now," Caswell said and turned wearily to the door. They stepped outside and he stopped in the hall, his expression bleak.

"Is he going to be all right?" Shotten asked, meaning Dan Gannon.

Caswell tried to straighten his clothing. "He'll never be all right, Mike. The drug's got him and there isn't any more. He killed Bessie, bless her sinful soul. He confessed that to me but he's paying for that." He looked at his watch and found that it had been broken in the scuffle. "My father gave me that if I promised not to take a drink before I was twenty-one. Kept my promise too, but on the night of my twenty-first birthday I got roaring drunk. That shows you how deceitful people are."

"You're a tough man, doc," Shotten said.

"If I wasn't," Caswell said, "I wouldn't be practicing medicine." He walked out and down the street and the clerk came up, his manner hesitating.

"Is Mr. Gannon all right?"

"Go ask him," McCaffey said.

"Did he—damage the room?"

"Wrecked it," Shotten said, and they left the place.

Captain Lovering arrived in town and expressed his regret at being delayed. He sat quietly while Shotten and McCaffey related Gannon's confession, and Lovering was satisfied.

"I can take this to court now," he said. "Linus, I suggest that you return to your duties without delay. I'll remain here and take care of the legal aspects of this matter."

"Yes, sir. Is Cochise at the mine?" Lovering nodded.

"Linus, let the boy go back with his people," Lovering said.

"I'm going to ask Cochise anyway," McCaffey said. "If you would, sir, ask Cochise to come to the doctor's house. The boy will have to translate."

"I'll do that," Lovering said. He got up and pulled on his gauntlets. "I'm damned glad to be getting on with army business. Shotten, did you see anything of that dispatch rider?"

"Private Noonan's carrying the dispatch case," Shotten said. "He's also with the escort for my wagons." He took out his watch and looked at it. "I've got to see Twilling and load up. Honestly, I haven't had a good rest since I started this work."

They parted and McCaffey remained on the street for a few minutes, then he walked over to the hotel and went to Dan Gannon's room. Gannon was trying to put on a clean shirt, but his hand was stiff from the bruised knuckles and his frustration was turning into a temper fit. He glared at McCaffey and said, "What do you want anyway?"

"Let me help you with that," McCaffey said. Gannon started to object, but he changed his mind and sat glumly while McCaffey buttoned the shirt and stuffed in the tail.

"Like a damned helpless baby," Gannon said dully. "You hate me, McCaffey. Why are you doing this?" He looked up. "Am I under arrest?"

"No, you're a free man. You shot Bessie and you're going to get away with it, as far as the law is concerned. But everyone will soon know that you killed her, and there won't be anyplace for you to go." He got a tie and tied it neatly. "You might even say that I'm dressing you for your funeral. You see, Doc Caswell's not going to give you any more morphine. You feel pretty good now, but in another six hours your belly will tie into knots and you'll go through the whole thing all over again." He stepped back and looked at Gannon. "Even with a tie on, you're a hell of a looking corpse."

"You're to blame for all this," Gannon said.

"Cuss your stupid ambitions. Cuss your belief that Dan Gannon is king. That's what to blame." He turned to the door and paused there. "I'm going back to the post. Goodbye, Gannon."

He threw a shoe at the closed door, but McCaffey was already walking down the hall and he didn't stop. Cutting across town, he went to Doctor Caswell's house and found him there with a bottle and a glass and a good glaze growing in his eyes.

"You're getting drunk," McCaffey said. "Is that going to help?"

"Nope, but I get drunk anyway, now and then. The boy was asking about you."

"Cochise is coming in. We're going to talk."

Caswell shook his head. "An Apache walking the street; that'll be something."

"There'll be soldiers with him," McCaffey said and went into the boy's room. Yazzi was sitting up in bed looking at a picture book Caswell had given him. He smiled and McCaffey put his hat on the bed. "Yazzi, I'm going back to the fort. Would you come with me?" He let the boy think about it for a moment. "I am speaking of your coming to stay, to live as my son."

"It is a great thing," Yazzi said. "But I must obey Cochise."

"Cochise will come to town before the sun sets and we will talk of it," McCaffey said. "But I wanted to tell you first, to give you a chance to make up your mind." He stood up and picked up his hat. "I'll be back, Yazzi."

He went through Caswell's office; the doctor was still sitting there but he had stopped drinking. "Damn you," Caswell said, "you stirred up my conscience."

"I should have kicked it."

By the time he arrived on the main street, Noonan and the other wagons with the escort detail had arrived and when Noonan saw McCaffey, he hurried over.

"By golly, sir, when you went with the Apaches, I

about gave you up for gone." He took off his kepi and flogged dust from his clothes. "Sure the hell a lot of people coming into the territory. Heading for the mountains, I guess. Some fella made a strike, I hear."

"Gold hunters?"

"Gold hunters and trouble hunters," Noonan said. "The Apaches ain't goin' to like it, sir, them prospectors rammin' around the mountains."

"Has the captain been told of this?"

"No, sir. I thought I'd get a drink before I delivered the dispatch case."

"You know better than that, Noonan," McCaffey said. "Just one drink?"

"Just a beer, sir."

"I think I'll go over to Twilling's store and watch them load wagons for five minutes. What you do in that time is your own business."

Noonan grinned, then ducked under the tie rail and went into the saloon. McCaffey went on down to the store, watched Shotten work his crew, then went back up the street. Noonan had come out of the saloon and was wiping the last of the suds from his lip when McCaffey drew abreast of him. He started to say something, then yelled loudly and gave McCaffey a shove that knocked him asprawl.

A .44 bellowed from the middle of the street and as he rolled, McCaffey saw Dan Gannon standing there, the pistol in his hand. He swung the gun, trying to pick up McCaffey in the sights, but Noonan grabbed his carbine and fired all in one sweeping motion and Gannon was spun back. He staggered, then crumpled, the pistol falling unfired from his fingers.

Men ran from the buildings and gathered in the street to look at him, and Noonan came up, the empty carbine still in his hands. He said, "I always wanted to shoot him too." He looked at McCaffey. "You hurt, sir? He had his pistol pointed right at you when I saw him. I didn't know if I'd shoved in time."

McCaffey fingered a rent in his shirt at the shoulder; the bullet had come that close to him. "You shoved just in time," McCaffey said. "Why don't some of you men get him off the street?"

"The army shot him," one man said. "Let the army clean it up."

"I'll see that it's taken care of, sir," Noonan said.

The shooting had attracted Shotten and he came through the crowd. He looked at Dan Gannon and said, "He hardly seems worth wasting a bullet on." Then he glanced at McCaffey. "I always said that I wanted to get him, but I'm glad someone else did it." Noonan came back with two enlisted men and a blanket and they gathered Dan Gannon in it and carried him off the street. The crowd began to break up and flies gathered in the blood in the dust.

McCaffey and Shotten walked over to some shade by a building and stood there. "The last time I saw Dan," Shotten said, "he was a big strapping man with two arms and the town pretty well in his pocket. But seeing him there in the street reminded me of one time when I saw a ship driven onto the rocks. A little pounding by the sea reduced it to fragments. Al's going to be a little lonely standing there on the scaffold waiting for the trap to be sprung. He was always jealous of Dan, but he really needed him. Twilling said that the captain's got Al and all the miners in the bullpen."

"There'll be a trial," McCaffey said. "But I really wonder what good it will do. Who'll stop the next man who comes along and wants it all for himself?"

"You," Shotten said. "Or someone like you. Me, maybe. I ain't so stupid that I can't learn from another man, Linus. You've taught me a few things, like not to let go of living just because I'd been hurt. I'm even thinking of finding me a woman now that I'm a respectable business man."

"There are few unattached women in Arizona."

"A man can always find what he looks for." He frowned. "Say, ain't that Cochise coming down the street? Times are sure changing, Apaches coming to town with soldiers. It's like finding a fox curled up asleep in the henhouse."

18

THEY RODE TOGETHER, the man and the boy, and the man smoked a cigar and listened to the boy chatter about his new haircut and his fine new blue jeans and checkered shirt, and at night they camped together and rode on at dawn.

When they reached the post, the guard passed on the word that McCaffey was back and they hardly had time to dismount in front of the main building when McCaffey's wife ran across the compound and threw herself in his arms. He kissed her in full view of the post, then put her down and said, "This is Yazzi. I've asked him to come and live with us."

She looked at the boy for a moment, then smiled and said, "Well, all right, but we'll have to look for bigger quarters. I think I'm pregnant."

He stared at her. "This is a devil of a time to tell a man that," he said and put his arm around her. "Take the boy along. I'll be along as soon as I can."

"Try to hurry," she said, smiling. "I've been waiting long enough."

He gave her waist a pinch and she pulled away quickly. "I think you've put on a pound or two," he said with a straight face.

"None of your patty fingers in public," she said and took Yazzi's hand.

McCaffey turned toward the door, then stopped for a look at his post. The population had increased considerably since he had left and a camp had been set up for the civilians passing through. They were all rough, solitary men in a hurry to get into the mountains and search for gold.

Sergeant Baker reported and brought McCaffey up to date on the status of the companies, the horses, and the small, close in patrol activity. Baker did not ask McCaffey what happened to him since he walked off the post, but he wanted to know and McCaffey felt that he was entitled to know; he offered Baker a chair and a cigar and filled him in on the details. McCaffey knew that the story would soon be circulated and he wanted Baker to have the straight of it.

"It'll be a relief to us, sir, having Cochise back with his people," Baker said. "They've been a restless lot these past weeks." He got up and put on his kepi. "All these civilians moving into the mountains ain't helped none either. The Apaches don't like it none and the civilians don't trust the Apaches. One of these days one or the other'll get killed and then you'll have a war started."

"We'll have to come up with a solution to it, sergeant," McCaffey said. "But in the meantime, I'm going to my quarters. I'll be here after evening mess. Report to me then and we'll put the post to bed."

"Yes, sir."

McCaffey left the building and hurried across the parade ground. Eloise was in the kitchen and Yazzi was perched on a stool. He said, "Your words are true, Mawcawpee. She is making sweet things for me in her fire."

"I've been wanting some gingersnaps," Eloise said. Then she smiled. "All right, so I'm pampering him. The contract surgeon arrived last week, Linus. He ought to change the dressing on Yazzi's leg."

"I'll get him to attend to it this evening," McCaffey said. He sat down and stretched his legs. "Each day you will spend several hours with books and will be taught to write and read well, Yazzi. In the afternoons you will ride with me and when you grow up you will know many things and people will say that you are a good man."

"I will do what pleases you, Mawcawpee," Yazzi said.

"Save the evenings for me," Eloise said and winked.

McCaffey stifled his smile. "That's getting pretty bold there, girl."

"I feel pretty bold," she said. "Are you going back to headquarters after supper?"

"For a bit," he said.

"Don't be long."

He smiled. "I won't." She took the cookies out of the oven and he picked up one and bounced it around in his hand until it cooled. Yazzi was more patient; he waited until he was served.

Then he took a bite and smacked his lips. "These are of great goodness," he said. "Better than those made by the woman with much fat."

Eloise laughed. "Who is that he's talking about?"

"Bessie," McCaffey said. "Yazzi, you were not told this, but Bessie is dead." The boy stopped eating and looked at McCaffey, and he put his arm around him. "Come in the other room and I'll tell you about it." He glanced at Eloise. "She befriended him. I'll tell you about it later." He led the boy into the other room, the cookies crumbled and forgotten in his clenched hand.

Captain Paul Lovering detailed the escorting job to Lieutenant Cleever, who made up in eagerness what he lacked in rank and experience. The prisoners, Al Gannon, and fourteen men, were herded together and guarded carefully by a squad of soldiers.

The other men who had been working for Gannon were released and advised to leave the territory, a suggestion in which many found considerable merit. They were a rough lot, long overdue for jail, and probably wanted in other parts of the country, but Lovering did not feel that he should make it a point to see that they got there.

He wanted the men who had held up the military wagons and killed the Indians, and he had them, confessions and all; all he had to do now was to see that they got to Prescott and jail to stand trial.

Lovering gave his instructions to Lieutenant Cleever,

then had Al Gannon brought over for a talk. Since his capture, a razor had been denied him, and Gannon sported a growing crop of whiskers.

"It is my intention to see you tried and hung," Lovering said. "However, I've given strict orders to shoot the first man who tries to break away while you're on the trail. Die you will, Mr. Gannon, by rope or lead."

"It's some distance to Prescott," Al Gannon said. "And I ain't dead yet. You won't get me like you got Dan; I won't be pulled into a trap."

"He made a fool play," Lovering said. "But I don't care to discuss it. Think what you damned please." He turned and walked over to where Lieutenant Cleever waited. "You may leave when ready, Mr. Cleever. Never relax your vigilance for a moment. They're all dangerous men."

"Yes, sir," Cleever said, and mounted his ten man detail. The prisoners were placed in wagons, chained securely, and Cleever turned them out on the town road.

That night he made camp by a waterhole and posted his guards and allowed the prisoners to eat four at a time, their hands free; armed troopers stood nearby, watching them, and as soon as they finished eating, they were chained and four more released.

Cleever was a careful man, too cautious; he liked to think over every move well in advance of making it. They had a four-day march to the Gila River, and things had been going so smoothly, so completely according to plan, that Cleever made his first mistake: he began to settle into an exact routine.

At the Gila, the first wagon crossed safely, but the second, containing Al Gannon, ran into trouble in midstream. Gannon and the seven men with him suddenly threw all their weight to one side, leaning far out, and the wagon capsized, spilling them into the water. One man surfaced and yelled, "We're drowning!"

Cleever's Christian instincts made him act and he ordered the sergeant to strike their chains. The sergeant rode into the river with a trooper beside him and before Cleever fully understood how it had happened, they had the sergeant off his horse, pulled him under, killed him, taken his pistol and carbine, killed the trooper, and broken free.

He immediately ordered the soldiers to take positions along the river bank, and they fired many rounds into the water as heads bobbed to the surface for air, but they only hit one man and that was not Al Gannon.

Yazzi was a bright boy who took pride in studying hard, and Lieutenant Skinner, who coached him in mathematics and history, told McCaffey that he was the best pupil he had ever had, which made Yazzi strut a bit. In two weeks, Yazzi had gone far in his multiplication tables, and endlessly recited them, in the morning, in the afternoon while he did his chores, and at the supper table, until Eloise began to tire of this mathematical perfection.

She had mixed feelings about the boy and it bothered her and she searched her heart for the truth. When she looked at him and saw his dark skin, walnut-colored eyes and high cheekbones, she could see the years ahead, the hard years where he would be an Indian living uninvited among the whites, loved in his own home, mistrusted or resented outside it. Perhaps, she thought, it's the child I'm carrying that makes me think these things, for she could see them growing up together, one white, one Indian.

She accepted the boy with her mind, but not her heart, and this was a constant prodding of her conscience and the more she tried, the further she came from a genuine love for him.

They had a late supper because Linus McCaffey had some heavy paperwork to take care of, and the meal was hurried for he had to go back; a patrol was expected in later and he wanted to talk to the officer about the civilians infiltrating the mountains for gold. The situation was growing bad; each week more men came, stayed briefly, and went on. The Apaches didn't like it. Twice Cochise had come to the post to speak of this and twice

McCaffey had put him off. But he couldn't do that for much longer.

Eloise was doing some sewing now, making clothes she would need later, and Yazzi was company for her; he liked to read from a story book that had been hers as a child, and he read it over and over again, carefully pronouncing his words and making childish, animated gestures to add zest to the tales.

At nine o'clock she made him take his bath, a twice weekly ritual, before going to bed. For a while she heard him stirring, then the house fell silent, save for the ticking of the clock. At ten she filled the lamp with coal oil because it was beginning to smoke. A bit later she heard the sentry call out and then the patrol came onto the post and she went to the door. The night was like ink and the only lights showing were at the guardhouse and headquarters. The sergeant dismounted his men and she turned back to her sewing.

She had taken only a few stitches when she heard a step on the porch and thought that it was Linus; the door opened and she turned and found Al Gannon standing there, dressed in a trooper's uniform. He pointed his pistol at her and said, "If you make a sound I'll blow your brains out."

Eloise put her sewing down and looked at him. He was not the man she remembered, for he was desperate now; there was a fire in his eyes that made him highly explosive. With surprising calm, she said, "Isn't that what you intend to do anyway?" She wondered if he could see any movement of her heart, for it hammered quite furiously.

"I want to kill both of you," he said softly. "He's got to come home. I'll wait."

"Only if I let you wait," she said. "You see, if I make you kill me now, the shot will wake the post. You won't have a chance to kill my husband."

He shook his head. "Lady, you wouldn't do that."

"What makes you think that I wouldn't? I love him that much."

He moved deeper into the room so he could see the

lamplight on her face. And he studied her awhile, then nodded. "Yes, I guess you'd do that."

He stood with his back to the bedroom door; she could partially see it, and a widening crack appeared and something in her face gave this away, for he whirled as Yazzi flung the door open and his nervousness made him fire. The bullet struck the frame and blew away a long splinter of wood; Yazzi held McCaffey's heavy cavalry pistol and he was trying to cock it with both thumbs, the heavy mainspring almost too much for him to overcome.

Al Gannon laughed and slip-hammered a shot at the boy, the bullet snipping past his head and breaking a pane of glass from the bedroom. Then Yazzi got the hammer eared back and let it go and the .44 boomed and Al Gannon's laugh was cut short.

He grunted and said, "Uuhh," and dropped his gun to clap both hands over the pain in his chest. He walked on legs turned lax and then his knees bent and hit the floor solidly. For a moment he remained that way, as though he were praying, then fell forward on his face.

Eloise and the boy ran to each other and they were hugging each other when McCaffey and a crowd from headquarters burst into the room.

Yazzi said, "I was asleep, Mawcawpee, and I heard his voice. It was the same voice I heard the night I listened at the house of the woman with much fat. I took your pistol from the holster, without permission, and for this I must be punished, but he was going to kill—"

Eloise held him tighter and kissed him and said, "Hush, hush, my brave little man. Hush now."

To a sergeant, McCaffey said, "Get him out of here." He spread his arms and turned the others to the door. "Thank you, gentlemen, everything's all right now."

He closed the door and put his arm around his wife and she turned to her chair, her hands shaking. "I saw the door open to the bedroom and I almost cried out for him to go back. Gannon fired at him twice while he was trying to cock the pistol." She shook her head and wiped tears from her eyes. "Linus, a dozen times I died over again while Yazzi stood there trying to cock that damned pistol."

"Some day, when I am a man," Yazzi said, "I will own a pistol. Is that not true, Mawcawpee?"

"It is true," McCaffey said gently. "You may light the fire and make coffee for us. Bring three cups."

The boy dashed into the kitchen, his nightshirt flapping, and he drew water, put the pot on the stove and went outside for wood; these busy sounds came to them in the other room.

"You've smiled at the boy," McCaffey said, "but what I saw when I opened the door was more than a smile. I can't describe the look I saw on your face. You had your eyes closed. Were you praying, Eloise?"

"Thanking God," she said, "for saving my son from death." She took his hand. "I don't want to take away his name, but perhaps we can give him another. Perhaps we could name him after my father."

"Sean? Let's make it American then. Call him John."

"John Yazzi McCaffey. I like it." She blew her nose. "I act like a fool sometimes, don't I?"

"Most of the time," he said, smiling. "But I like it."

She raised her head and looked at him. "Linus, he was wearing a uniform. How do you suppose he got it?"

"Off one of the men who were guarding him," he said. "I don't know, really. Just guessing. He probably waited for a patrol to come along, and the night was dark; it would be hard to spot an extra man. The sentry would pass him onto the post without question." He bent and kissed her. "Don't worry about it. Don't even care."

"Yes, it's through and done with," she said. "Perhaps now you can spend more time on the post. I don't like it when you're away so much."

He laughed softly. "You're liable to see so much of me now that you'll wish I'd go on patrol." He pulled her to her feet and put his arms gently around her. "Are we going to stay up all night?"

19

CAPTAIN LOVERING arrived in the early morning and he met McCaffey at headquarters. The reports McCaffey had carefully prepared had bypassed the captain enroute, so he was brought up to date on Al Gannon's death.

"A messy business concluded," Lovering said, puffing his cigar. "Cleever resigned his commission. The only decent thing he could do under the circumstances. Four of Gannon's men were captured. One was killed trying to break into a store for supplies, and the others skipped the country." He laughed. "You say the Indian boy shot him?"

"My son shot him, yes," McCaffey said.

Lovering's eyebrow went up. "How's that working out?"

"Fine," McCaffey said. He switched the subject. "I expect, sir, that you've come with new orders for me."

"I have for a fact," Lovering said. "Frankly, Department is disturbed about these civilians moving into the Apache country. Sooner or later someone's going to crack a cap in anger and we'll have another outbreak. The general suggested to me, in a dispatch, that I establish a reservation on the San Carlos and move the Apaches there."

McCaffey reared out of his chair. "My God, sir, that's impossible!"

"Exactly my sentiments," Lovering said, drawing slowly on his cigar; he seemed most pleased with himself. "Which is why I'm putting you in command of the whole operation. Simply build the reservation buildings in two months and move all the Apaches on it. Indian agent and personnel will arrive in late summer." He smiled. "By the way, your promotion came through."

"To hell with the pro—" He seemed shocked. "It did?"

"Yes, I couldn't have a second lieutenant in charge of such an undertaking."

"Captain, this whole thing is completely impossible!"

"I'm sure it is, but somehow you'll manage. Don't look so crestfallen, Linus. Merely regard it as temporary duty."

"Thank you, sir," McCaffey said dryly. "You've taken a burden from my mind."

"I'm sure I have," Lovering said and got up to stretch his legs. "Invite me to supper, Linus. Your wife's a wonderful cook. And I want to take a look at this son of yours." He put his arm around McCaffey's shoulders. "After all, we may get this boy appointed to the Academy one day. Tradition, you know. A man's oldest goes to the Academy."

When they stepped outside, McCaffey said, "Captain, would you explain my new duties to my wife? She's pregnant and if I have to be away from the post for weeks at a time—"

"Glad to," Lovering said, smiling. "After all, I'm leaving in the morning."